Originally from Warwickshire, Gavin now lives on the Welsh Borders where village life allows him more time to devote to writing.

From an early career working with the disabled, Gavin moved into retail with the development of his own woodcraft supplies company. With a background in a wide range of pursuits, Gavin's novels reflect his love of the countryside, a fondness for mysteries and adventure, and a long association with feral cats that has given him a unique perspective on human nature.

The Un-familiar Cat

Gavin Rees-Jones

The Un-familiar Cat

Nightingale Books

A CIP catalogue record for this title is
available from the British Library.

ISBN 978 1 907552 17 5

Nightingale Books is an imprint of
Pegasus Elliot MacKenzie Publishers Ltd.
www.pegasuspublishers.com

First Published in 2011

Nightingale Books
Sheraton House Castle Park
Cambridge England

Printed & Bound in Great Britain

Contents

INTRODUCTION
Silas, Last Wizard of Barren Moor

'If that cat could talk.' A phrase often spoken in jest but to anyone tempted to repeat it, be careful of what you wish ... it may just come true.

Silas Grimdyke was the last of his kind, the very last in a long, long line of white wizards ... or so he believed. Unfortunately, what Silas did not yet know, was that the magic had actually run out many years earlier and the once great wizarding line of Grimdyke had ended with his father, Ethan.

Silas' strange tale began when he was handed the keys to Highfell Croft and more importantly for Silas, the keys to the potions cupboard. On his twenty-first birthday, Silas officially took over the family business and became a wizard. However, as the special day approached, his only thoughts were firmly focussed on the inheritance he stood to gain and not the great responsibility that came with it. As far as Silas could see, his entire legacy amounted to little more than a small rusty cauldron that leaked badly, a large and ancient spell book that he had never been able to understand and a black cat ... a very unhappy and slightly smelly black cat, called Nightfire. As his father had long suspected, Silas was unable to see past the shabby appearance of his legacy to the important gift he actually stood to receive.

To make matters worse, Silas was not exactly a friendly person and he only saw magic as a way of improving his own lot. In particular, his wealth and standing in the community.

Therefore, it came as no great surprise that on the day he assumed his father's role, his first act was one of pure selfishness. Watched by a new and more optimistic young cat, a change Silas failed to notice, his first act was to attempt to turn the blocks of peat, cut and gathered for burning in the croft hearth, into bars of gold. Unfortunately for Silas, he chose to demonstrate his new powers in front of not only his doubting new familiar, Raven, but also the whole of the assembled villagers. The villagers of nearby Skellside had in fact turned out in their droves to welcome the new wizard. As keen friends of the retired wizard, Ethan, they had high hopes for his son and as this was to be the first spell from their new mage, they watched in eager anticipation.

Silas drew back the sleeves of his robes in preparation, whilst eying the crowd carefully to be sure he had their full attention.

'Chrysopea!' he called out grandly and he waved his crooked hemlock wand at the pile of dusty peat blocks.

Raven closed his green eyes and waited for the bang. Despite the extra flourish Silas had given his wand, nothing happened, apart that is from someone at the back of the room sniggering. There was no flash, no loud bang, nothing; just a few spiders, which fell to the floor after Silas had dislodged them from their webs in the ceiling with his wand. Silas muttered and grumbled something short and very rude into his unkempt beard. He tended to swear and mumble a lot, he even managed to say a few things that made Raven blush. Silas decided that there was nothing else for it; he would have to try something else and quickly, before he lost any more respect in his audience's eyes. The inability to make himself instantly rich was a serious setback for Silas and he realised that he would need to work on the spell and the next time, without onlookers. Just then, something else occurred to him, a sort of consolation prize.

With the crowd rapidly growing impatient and increasingly sceptical, he turned his attention to the pitchers of water standing on the kitchen table. Because the old croft had no mains water supply, all drinking water had to be collected from a spring in the garden, after which it was left in large stone jugs for use later. Silas quickly came up with a new plan. The thought had occurred to him that if he could not be rich, at least he could be merry and so he cast a spell to turn the water into beer.

'Aqua-fermentum!'

This second and even more grandly delivered spell also failed spectacularly, leaving Silas with nothing more than embarrassment and a room full of sniggering onlookers. All things considered, Silas' first day as a wizard had been an abysmal disaster and in his ensuing fury, he promptly banished the villagers from ever setting foot on his land again. For fourteen years, they would be magically prevented from disturbing his solitude. Of course, in choosing to ban them for fourteen years, Silas had simply taken the magical number, seven and doubled it for good luck … *his*, not theirs. As far as Silas was concerned, at least this spell appeared to be more successful. Seeing the villagers leaving his croft in some hurry, convinced Silas of his mastery of at least one of the darker spells. Unbeknown to Silas the reason for his apparent success was far simpler. The people of the village had seen quite enough to show them that Silas was not the great wizard his father had been and as a result, they could see no use for such a greedy and bad tempered failure. Staying away from Highfell Croft would be their pleasure.

So there it was, almost his first act on becoming the official village wizard had been to curse the whole hamlet. Furthermore, not satisfied with banishing them he later summoned rain and harsh winters to plague them for fourteen years. However, on Barren Moor, the high ground that bordered the village, the weather was frequently wet and dreary so the villagers had become accustomed to harsh winters over the years and did not notice the change, if indeed there had been one. Silas however took this as another indication of his superior spell-casting ability and as such, another result for darker magic.

This day was to mark a serious turning point for Silas when he took a decision that would scar him for the rest of his life. It was on this day that Silas decided that if good magic were beyond him he would turn his back on it and end the once proud and good Grimdyke line by becoming a dark warlock.

CHAPTER ONE
The Old Village

Having successfully cut himself off from the villagers, the only company left to Silas was his cat and it is with the Grimdyke familiars that the *real* story begins. To understand how Raven came to be stuck with such an unpleasant and incompetent fellow, we really need to leave Silas for a moment and look back more than a hundred years in time to the first Grimdyke familiar, and where this curious relationship began.

In the neighbouring valley, on the far side of HighFell Ridge, lies another large expanse, known as Greyfell Moor. This wet and harsh moor of peat bog, stream and reed bed spreads out from the foot of Highfell Ridge as far as the neighbouring Greyfell Pike. It is this second smaller ridge of bleached limestone that gives its name to the flowing carpet of purple, green and brown hues that nestles between.

Long abandoned by all but wild animals, the hills and mountains around Greyfell Moor once supported a thriving community, a small village of mineworkers and their families. In its heyday, the village was a match in size for Skellside and boasted a number of shops as well as a small inn called "The Lode of Mischief". The hills around the village once grumbled and banged to the sounds of rocks being excavated as miners sought the precious metal ore contained within the hillside. Workers' houses grew up alongside the processing sheds and light railway sidings and a prosperous village quickly spread along the valley sides. As mine workers pursued the ore deeper into the hills, large spoil heaps of excavated rock began to grow on the landscape, disfiguring the natural beauty of the hillside. Rivers and streams were dammed and their water harnessed to drive the large wheels that supplied power to the industry. Later, steam engines replaced these natural power sources and production soared. As the mine output reached its peak, disaster struck the community. The ore suddenly ran out and despite the best efforts of the company surveyors to find new deposits, the veins of precious ore had been exhausted and the mines were quickly abandoned.

Scarred limestone escarpments, and the network of tunnels and mineshafts that ran deep inside the hillside, are now all that remain of the once bustling industry. Slowly the spoil heaps began to grass over as plants reclaimed the land. The streams soon overran the dams to return to their natural course but there was one other legacy left behind by the retreating workers, one that in their haste they had overlooked. It was of course, the miners' cats.

When the mines and processing plants closed down, the workers left the area but not so their feline friends. Their original role had been to keep vermin away from the cottages, stores and processing sheds. In their time, they had saved the mining company hundreds of pounds each year by guarding the food stocks against the voracious appetites of the local rodent population. However, when the workers left to seek employment elsewhere, the cats suddenly found themselves alone and unwanted.

Hoping in vain for the miners' return, they hung around the old buildings for years after the closure. Long after the crofts and workshops had fallen into disrepair, they continued to wait for their owners' homecoming but none ever came. Eventually, as the discarded food finally ran out and the buildings began to crumble and fall, the cats were forced to move on.

Turning away from the hillside they knew and towards the bleak moors, they sought shelter and a new life without humans. Just beyond the cluster of industrial buildings, on the fringes of Greyfell Moor itself, lay a small croft. The blacksmith and farrier, who once cared for the mine ponies, had occupied this small dwelling but now it too lay derelict. In their day, the hardworking pit ponies that pulled the ore carts had once wandered the moor. There, they would spend their time feeding on the sparse grasses and resting between shifts in the mine. They were tended to by the smith and his family who tried to make their hard lives a little more comfortable. The smith kept the ponies shod and well fed and if they were unwell, he sought the advice of the Skellside wizard, Grimdyke. Like the miners' cottages, the croft and forge now lay abandoned by the mining company but it did not lie empty. Greyfell Colony, as the abandoned cats became known, now lived in the old smithy and it was they that foraged on the moors now in place of the ponies. The future for them as ferals looked as bleak as the moor itself but it was all they had.

Some years later, Ezra Grimdyke left his home to take a long walk over the moors. He missed the regular visits from the farrier and decided that a trip down memory lane might ease him. Ezra could see the old abandoned, tumbled-down cottages of the mineworkers' village and he recalled how busy and bustling the area had once been. It brought back many pleasant memories for him but after a few minutes of wandering between the old buildings and recalling friends long-gone, he turned to head for home. It was at this point that something made Ezra choose a different pathway back. It could have been the memory of his old friend the farrier or something new that Ezra did not quite understand, but he turned to follow the abandoned branch of the trackway that led away from the village. The old wizard had always relied on his instincts and when they told him to take a certain path, he usually listened.

As he walked, it suddenly dawned on him that he was following the old track bed that once carried the light railway and instead of the path home, he was on the branch line that led to his old friend's forge.

'They were hard times, but hard times often forge strong friendships.'

At the other end of this small branch sat the smithy and the place where the ponies once grazed. Memories of the forge and of the moorland dotted with hungry ponies, flooded back to Ezra but when he rounded the bend, he was in for a quite a shock. The small house and forge building now lay derelict. Ezra stopped and thought:

'Has it really been that long?' and then he sighed. 'They say that not all change is bad but I shall miss my old friend ... and the ponies.'

At that moment, Ezra got the distinct feeling that he was not so alone after all. He cautiously withdrew the wand that he always carried with him. He kept it tucked inside his jacket where it was always ready, should he feel the need. Ezra stood quite still. Whoever ... *whatever* was watching him he could sense they were no threat. The old wizard had powers his occasional visitors could only guess at but they knew him of old and had trusted the family of Grimdyke for many years. Ezra held out his hand towards the old smithy and closed his eyes.

'Now I see you ...' Then he began to count. 'Yan, tan, tether, mether, pip, azer, sezar ...' Ezra counted as the old shepherds had once done. He counted as he felt the many pairs of eyes watching him. Each time he reached 'jigget' or twenty, he would bend over a finger and begin again. 'So many of you!' Ezra said softly. 'But there's no need to be afraid of me.'

Having counted a worrying number of eyes, Ezra made a gesture with his hand as if wiping it across a misty window to clear the pane.

'Ah, there you all are!'

One by one, amongst the sedge and reeds, heads began to appear and tails flicked. One by one, the colony of miners' cats came to investigate their new visitor. Stopping short of actually standing next to Ezra, a group of older cats took up position on the turf bank just in front of him. A large black and white tom then stepped forward a little and sniffed at the air.

'I hope you find nothing too unpleasant, I did wash this morning!' Ezra explained.

The cat then took another few steps forward and Ezra knelt down on one knee and held out the back of his hand for the inquisitive tom to sniff. Whatever the cat detected appeared to satisfy its curiosity and he proceeded to walk all around Ezra, rubbing his shoulder against him as he circled.

'I take it that I meet with your approval.' The old wizard smiled. 'My name is Ezra and I think we have something to talk about.'

The black and white tom then sat down at Ezra's feet and while the other cats washed and preened between listening, Ezra talked about their situation. As he spoke, it was as if the old gent could actually understand the mews and meows the tom made in response and for his part, the tom appeared to listen to Ezra intently.

'I quite understand your reluctance to leave my friend ... I really do but ...'

'Eoww!'

'Quite right,' Ezra replied, 'you're quite right. This is your home now but still I feel that I should help somehow.'

Feeling sorry for the cats but clearly unable to care for them all, Ezra Grimdyke, being the kind-hearted gent he was, decided to cast a powerful spell over Greyfell Moor. The enchantment would banish forever all that would prey on the cats and ensure a plentiful supply of food and water for them, for as long as they wished to live there. Once again, he withdrew his old rowan wand and turned to face the moors.

'Semper-tutamen!' Ezra said firmly and with his wand, he traced the shape of a sideways eight in the air.

From the tip of his wand, a bright electric-blue light burst forth and, spreading across the moor like a tidal wave, it rushed over the land to envelop it. The flash of metallic blue continued to roll until it had passed over the entire valley at which point, an eerie silence fell over the land. After a brief pause, the moors came back to life again and the sound of crickets and birdsong filled the air. The cats on the turf bank looked first at Ezra before looking towards the moor. They sniffed at the air, something was different and they were aware that something had changed. More cats then appeared from the old buildings to congregate along the bank until quite a crowd had gathered.

'I'm very pleased to finally meet you all.' Ezra smiled and then he bowed low and long to the assembled colony. 'I hope my small contribution meets with your approval.'

The cats then climbed down from the bank to form a large group on the track-way in front of him. They meowed, chattered and chirruped to each other and as they did, they wound around fellow cats as the group talked. Ezra waited patiently as the debate continued and for a while, and not wishing to eavesdrop, he simply sat quietly on a large limestone boulder by the side of the trackway. There Ezra took in the sounds and smells of the moor and as the sensations took his mind to another time, he tried hard not to eavesdrop on their deliberations.

The cats, all but the old black and white tom, then returned to the bank of turf and a few seconds later, a lithe and glossy black-coated female cat pushed her way through them to stand in front of Ezra. She deposited at his feet a stunned and very worried looking mouse. Apart from being terrified by the whole experience, this gift was intact and relatively unharmed. Ezra bent down to stroke the cat's head. At first, she backed away but after lowering her head as far as she could to avoid his touch, she finally agreed to one quick rub. Ezra thanked her for the gift and for her trust, before picking up the tiny offering by the scruff of its neck. Much to the colony's surprise, he then passed his wand over the creature as it shook and trembled between his fingers, after which the brown field mouse was seen to turn snow white. To the colony's even greater surprise, he then popped the creature into his top pocket, instead of his mouth as they had expected. Ezra explained.

'Forgive me, and it is no criticism of your way of life, in fact the thought is very much appreciated. It's just that I need companionship at the moment far more than lunch.'

Meows and chattering broke out along the bank and moments later, the young, jet-black female cat stepped forward again, this time to join the old man on his journey home. Although naturally wary of humans, she had been impressed by the wizard's understanding of their language but more than that, she was curious about what had become of her gift, the small mouse.

In gratitude for their protection from predators and a regular supply of food, the colony of cats elected to provide the Grimdyke household with a succession of familiars, for both protection and companionship. Because as they pointed out to Ezra before he left, a wizard without a cat may be mistaken for a fool with a small stick but a wizard with a familiar at his side may become all that he is and in the case of the Grimdykes of old, that meant a very powerful wizard indeed.

CHAPTER TWO
Partners

The long and honourable wizarding family of Grimdyke had always been there to help the people of the area. They cured illnesses, in both villagers and their livestock alike, warned them of dangers to come and later as the world changed, even started cars for them when all else had failed. In gratitude of the wizard's continuing friendship and help, the villagers regularly left gifts of food and clothes at his door. It was always considered an honour if the wizard chose *your* handmade cloak to wear or your lovingly knitted gloves were seen keeping his hands warm on a cold, bleak day. These gifts supported the wizard and his family, and helped to supplement the food they grew in the croft gardens.

As their part of the arrangement, the cats decided that every seventh year, they would send their strongest and blackest born, to live with the wizard's family as his familiar. The arrangement allowed the returning cat to train a suitable replacement, which took seven long years and started almost from the day of birth with the chosen candidate. The apprenticeship proper, with the wizard, lasted for another seven years after which the cat would return to begin training another replacement. So the cats always worked one familiar in hand and as the retiring cat returned to the colony, a replacement trained by the previous familiar, would leave for the wizard's croft, allowing the returning cat to train the next "chosen one". This way there was always a new familiar ready and waiting to take over, ensuring both an unbroken line of companions for the wizard and contact with him for the colony. This arrangement quickly established a strong bond between the colony and the wizarding family, to become an arrangement they were to enjoy for many, many years.

As tradition dictated, on the seventh night, of the seventh month, of the seventh year, the outgoing familiar would slip un-noticed from the croft to make the long and arduous journey back to the colony, scenting the route as he travelled. On his return, he would explain the route to his replacement and as the new cat would leave for the croft and his new life with the Grimdykes, the retiring cat would then be introduced to his young apprentice.

This is the point at which our story really begins. The cat about to retire was called Nightfire and by the time of his return, the colony had already chosen and trained his lucky replacement, Luna. From amongst the litters born seven years earlier, Luna had been chosen and trained and now eagerly awaited his instructions and the all-important directions to the wizard's cottage. When Nightfire duly arrived at the colony he found a strong young tom, keen and bright eyed, watching out for him. This strong kit was to be his apprentice. After Nightfire and the young Raven had been introduced to each other, Nightfire left briefly to talk with his own replacement, Luna. Nightfire passed to Luna his instructions for the long journey and Luna memorised the scent he should follow across the moors to the wizard's croft. As Luna left for his new life, Nightfire entered the colony with Raven at his side.

Fourteen years earlier, when Nightfire had been chosen, he had been an easy choice for the colony as his wily nature and sleek black coat made him a natural for a familiar. Nightfire had one other rare quality that made him very special: he was born with red eyes that lit up like flames in the dark. Only very rarely in many centuries was a cat so blessed and as a result, great things were expected of Nightfire. For his part, Nightfire had learned his role well and had gone on to form a special bond with the old wizard, Ethan. Sadly, this was much to the annoyance of Ethan's son, Silas, who as an attention seeking youth, began to suspect that his father preferred the cat to him. Silas was blinded by his jealousy and it proved a bitter seed that was to take root and grow between Silas and his father. The bond between familiar and wizard *is* very special but sadly, it was a connection the young Silas failed to understand.

At the end of his time with Ethan, Nightfire had one last duty to perform and just seven short years in which to complete the task. He had to teach the eager Raven all he needed to know about his new duties as familiar but unbeknown to either Nightfire or Raven, age and infirmity were to persuade Ethan to relinquish his position to his son, Silas, earlier than he would have wished. Raven was not only being prepared for a new role but a new master.

In the years that followed as Luna settled into his new role with Ethan, Nightfire could not help thinking that Raven was if anything, a little too keen. He would often rush his lessons, always wanting to know what came next. It was an unfortunate trait and one he would have in common with his new master. While he was with Ethan, Nightfire had sensed Silas' eagerness to wield the magic wand but his intentions were so different to those of his master. It was this sense of foreboding that had made Nightfire uncomfortable and it still left him with a feeling in his tail that he simply could not shake off. It also made him determined to do his very best to prepare Raven for whatever was to come. To do that successfully, he would need to put his doubts about him to one side and concentrate on his training. After all, Raven *was* the chosen one and when the time was right, the changeover would take place as dictated by tradition. Nightfire could only hope that Luna had found Ethan still wielding the wand when he turned up at the croft to take his place and not a young and impatient Silas.

Skipping through his instructions with all the eagerness of youth, Raven barely heard a word of Nightfire's instructions. His head was already filled with tales of magic and mystery. In fact, he could already smell the smoke that accompanied a spell well cast and see the flash of light as the magic took hold. However, Nightfire was patient and he could still remember his own eagerness to do his bit for the colony when he was a young kit but since then he had learned much, far more than he had ever expected to learn. Ethan was a kindly wizard and as his familiar, Nightfire had shared in his knowledge of spells and incantations. He learned about herbs and their healing powers, their use in potions and the correct movement of the wand to create the precise flourish needed for each spell. Although he had found it nearly impossible to hold the wand himself, he practised with a small twig of mountain ash that he had pulled from the besom broom in the kitchen. Nightfire would never be a wizard like Ethan, after all, it was not his role but amongst his skills, he did learn how to stun a mouse from fifty paces and how to turn clothes pegs into chicken nuggets … he liked the clothes peg trick the best.

Nightfire's role and that of his many predecessors had been to protect the wizard. He had to warn him of any encroaching danger, of changes in fortune to come and ward off minor irritations that might distract his master. All these things he now attempted to instil into Raven but all he ever got in return was half of Raven's attention, the rest he would spend on daydreams and wishful thinking.

Over the next seven years as Raven grew into a strong fighter and keen hunter, Nightfire taught him some of the finer points of a familiar's life. He wanted to show him that confrontation was not the only way and that negotiation and planning could often help a familiar avoid unnecessary fights.

Fighting was a last resort and betrayed a lack of real imagination. As Nightfire reminisced, Raven *half* listened to the tales about the nearby village and the people who lived there. He was told about their frequent visits to the croft and of how the villagers brought gifts for Ethan. At the same time, they usually remembered to bring a few treats for him too, leftover titbits and ends off the Sunday roast. Between offerings from the villagers and the odd chicken clothes peg, he hardly ever had to hunt at all during his time with the wizard, at least not for food but there were other things on the moors besides prey. Nightfire had even seen some of them with his own eyes.

Jack-o-lanterns that danced across the bogs, the great Barghest, a foul black dog-like beast that roamed the moor on moonless nights, Bogles, malevolent spirits that broke machinery and blighted crops ... or worse. Ethan had explained them all to Nightfire but more importantly, he explained how to deal with them. Then Nightfire mentioned to Raven, the Cat Sidhe, a rare visitor from the far north. This was a large and powerful cat faery, one that could take human form or vanish completely from sight if it so wished. Raven was not at all sure about this particular creature. It seemed to him that its behaviour betrayed catlife, as he knew it. Why would any cat want to look like a human? It was a riddle too far for Raven but all the same, he wanted to know more about the mysterious Cat Sidhe. Nightfire cleverly used his interest in the legend to introduce Raven to more of the things he needed to master before he could take his place at the wizard's side and slowly Raven learned, despite his impatience. Raven learned about potions, second sight, scent trails and the stars, he also learned to fight and track. As the time drew near, Nightfire moved on to the more difficult aspects of his training and crossed his claws that Raven would listen and take it in.

'If you see your enemy approaching, what should you do?'

Raven was all for fighting but when his suggestion did not find immediate favour with his mentor, he tried another approach.

'Run, run for the nearest and highest tree?'

'And what if there are no high trees or your retreat alerts the enemy to your presence? What if, in your haste, you snap a dry twig under your paw or your scent is brushed against a clump of reeds, what then of your chances?'

'I'm dog food?'

'At the very least ... or it could be *far* worse. Think ... use your brain. You hide! Your ears are acute, your eyes almost unrivalled in the dark and your sense of smell outmatched by few. You should withdraw and watch. Make no sound, chatter not, instead just watch. Only act when you are sure of success.'

'When do I get to turn rocks into roast chickens?'

'When Ethan shows you how, that is when! Your loyalty up to now has been to your colony. When you join the wizard, you must show him the same loyalty, for his family saved our kind and sought no reward. This is why they *must* be rewarded ... by our friendship and protection.'

Raven's training continued and Nightfire taught him all he could, at least while Raven would listen. When the seventh night, of the seventh month, of the seventh year finally came around Nightfire had done all he could to prepare his young apprentice, the rest was up to him.

Probably the only thing Raven paid full attention to was the directions he was given on how to reach his new home. It would never do to turn up late on one's first day at work or worse still, fail to turn up at all! Therefore, when Luna returned after seven years' happy service with his master Ethan, Raven was beside himself with anticipation and with the scent fresh in his nostrils and a full moon overhead, he set off for Highfell Croft. As Luna watched Raven bound away into the night to take his place, he had a few words of concern to pass on to Nightfire.

'The old wizard is tired. He talks of retiring.'

'But I understood the son was to carry on the family line.'

'Ethan is training his son, Silas, but he does not have the understanding of his father. I fear for the future and also what Raven will face.'

'The family of Grimdyke has always been a good and honourable line. I am sure the son, when he takes over, will turn out to be just like his father.'

'I hope you're right Nightfire or Raven is in for a very rough time!'

'All we can do now is wait and keep our claws crossed, besides, you will have your paws full with training the next familiar … when the colony has chosen. The kits arrived a little late this season.'

CHAPTER THREE
Arrival

Despite the many perils along the way, Raven duly arrived at Highfell Croft, an eager replacement for the outgoing Luna, but sadly his enthusiasm for the task ahead was not to last. His passion for the craft was quickly to be replaced with resignation and then finally, disappointment. Ethan Grimdyke was already in the process of handing over the family business to Silas when Raven arrived. At first, he thought that he would have the luxury of two masters to serve but it became quickly apparent that something was very wrong with the situation.

To both his credit and later his shame, Raven began to see something of himself in the young, would-be wizard. Despite the patience shown to him by his father, Silas always wanted more and sooner. Even before an incantation had been learned and mastered, Silas was thinking about the next one. Before a transformed glass of water could be further turned into a cup of tea that actually tasted like tea, Silas was thinking about coffee.

'When do we get on to the good stuff?' Silas would often demand.

'When you can tell it from the bad!' Ethan would reply.

Silas usually responded by flicking his badly chosen hemlock wand and casually shattering a chair or some other piece of furniture in the croft. Ethan sighed and then he patiently repaired the splintered chair with a gesture from his wand and a few well-chosen words, always being careful to keep the secret from Silas, until he was ready. Even at this early stage, Ethan was a worried man. If Silas did not carry on the family tradition, it would mark the end of the Grimdyke wizarding line.

'With the way Silas is shaping-up maybe that's not such a bad thing ... but what then of the villagers? I cannot let them down or betray our promise to the cats. Who knows how long the enchantment will last without a Grimdyke at Highfell Croft.'

Ethan struggled on with his churlish son and Raven did what he could to help, mainly for the sake of his master.

The small croft that was home to Ethan, Silas and Raven lay on the opposite side of the moor to the small village and in contrast to Skellside, Highfell Croft usually lay in the shadow of Highfell Ridge. Separating the two, the aptly named Barren Moor supported little plant or animal life and was even devoid of trees much higher than a man's waist. It was white with deep, drifting snow in winter, and wet and boggy in summer. It was a most inhospitable place but curiously appropriate for Silas. The look on his face perfectly reflected the look of the moors on a damp, drizzly day. In contrast, when the weather was fine and the sun shone, Ethan would often walk out onto his beloved moors and the brightness of his smile and the twinkle in his eye would be reflected in the joy and abundant life that always shone through when Ethan was there.

'Barren Moor ... what's in a name?' he would say, 'Nowhere is barren if you know where and how to look.'

There is a pleasure to be found in simple things but it is a skill rarely appreciated by the young and one that can even be lost to the old, in trying times. Ethan never lost the ability to look at a damp, soggy bog and see the dragonflies and the newts. He could look at the sun-bleached limestone pavements and see the bright purple thrift growing in the cracks between the rocks and the bees that flitted from flower to flower. Even in Silas, he could see the good but whether he could reach it or not was unknown, even to Ethan. He had to give Silas the opportunity to prove himself but if all his efforts failed, what then? What he really needed was a plan 'B' but that was proving to be something he was unable to conjure-up, at least so far.

Ethan persisted for years with Silas, teaching him how to heal broken bones in animals, cure plants of blight and find lost keys or mobile phones when the villagers began to lose all hope. However these were not the spells that Silas most wanted and to his annoyance, it appeared that his father was not about to divulge them to him any day soon. This forced Silas to play the long game. He knew that one day, when Ethan finally handed over the keys to the potions cupboard, that he would be able to get his hands on the family spell book. All he had to do was bide his time. In the meantime, poor Raven would be forced to dodge the frequent bad spells that came crackling and hissing in his direction, having being carelessly cast by his master's son. All the time he was thinking about when Ethan would leave and Silas would take over as his new master.

'This is not what I signed up for!' Raven muttered bitterly as he cast his own small spell to douse the smouldering patch of fur on his tail. 'I did my bit, I learned how to be a good familiar ... well most of it! It's not my fault Silas is a complete and utter dog-t ...'

'RAVEN! Raven where are you?' It was the voice of his master.

Raven duly appeared at his master's feet where he wound in and out of his legs.

'Ah Raven my good friend. I know these have been somewhat trying times for you ... they haven't exactly been a walk in the park for me either!' Ethan chuckled dryly. 'He's a good boy at heart but I fear he has no sense of ... *direction* and I'm afraid ... well, just between the two of us, I'm a little afraid of how he might turn out!'

Raven was shocked. He had never thought his master would give up on Silas, despite his clear lack of talent.

'It forces me to do something I'm not entirely happy about.' At this point Raven sighed. 'It's not something I *want* to do just something I *must*.' Hearing this Raven pulled himself together and prepared for the worst. 'I must hand the reins over to Silas sooner than I would have liked.'

'He's going to put me in reins?'

'No, he's not, relax! He's not *that* bad, besides he doesn't know the spell!' As Ethan sat in the large wooden rocking chair, Raven climbed on his lap. He could sense that there would be few times like this ahead and if he were alone with Silas, he would need to be on his guard all the time. Raven purred and Ethan rubbed his chin and then Ethan explained.

'I have to hope that the responsibility will snap him out of his selfish ways ... I know what you're thinking, why don't I cast a spell on him to improve his behaviour. Well, I'm also sure that you already know the answer to that one.'

'No personal gain or controlling another person's will, right?'

'Right! I'm telling you all this now because I hope you will forgive me for what I am about to do.'

'He's going to send me to a cattery!'

'You know me better than that ... although you seem to be forgetting that I know what you're thinking ... *most* of the time!' Ethan ran his wand over Raven's back to relieve an itch he could sense building there. This made Raven purr even more loudly.

'I guess I've just been around Silas too long, sorry master!'

'Well I'm afraid you'll be spending a lot more time with him. It's time he took over the family business. Besides, I have one last job I must complete and to do it I need him here, looking after things at Highfell.'

Ethan got up again and Raven retreated to his favourite seat in the house, the windowsill overlooking the moor. There he could watch the comings and goings of the people of the village and the occasional stray bird amongst the bracken. It was also a quiet place to think.

The small footpath that led from the wizard's croft across Barren Moor to the village on the other side was a well-trodden path and one used by young and old alike. That was until Silas took over and began putting visitors off with his wayward attempts to cast spells. Lately the path had become overgrown and the way little used, except by the curious.

Time eventually came for Ethan to hand over the keys of the croft to Silas and in a completely unemotional farewell, Ethan left, without further word of explanation as to where he was going or if he would ever return. The only thing he said to Silas was ...

'Take care of Raven in my absence. I shall hear of any cruelty towards him!'

Silas nodded his grudging agreement with his father's wishes. Then Ethan was gone, across the moor and off to the village of Skellside and an awaiting taxi. Silas looked to his hands and the large bunch of keys he had been given. Then he headed straight for the potions cupboard.

This brings us back to the scene a few days after Silas' failed attempts to impress the villagers, and their subsequent banishment from his land.

For a while, all grew quiet again. The people largely forgot about Silas, choosing instead to remember his father, Ethan and declare how sorely he was missed. Children hoping to get a glimpse of the "angry hermit", as Silas had become known, would venture in small groups across the moor and along the path to the croft. Silas would rant at them from the doorway and shout all kinds of made-up nonsense spells at them. They never worked of course, much to the further frustration of Silas.

Day by day, Silas grew more bitter and angry over his lack of wizarding power and Raven became the unwilling subject of his many failed attempts to cast spells. Normally, a wizard would show the good sense to cast a spell of protection over his familiar before attempting any such dangerous enchantments but unfortunately for Raven, his new master had not been up to the task. When properly cast, such a spell would reward the familiar with strength and make him practically impervious to harmful magic. It also has the added advantage of suspending aging. Therefore, a familiar would be exactly the same age when he left the wizard's company, as he was when he arrived at Greyfell but he would certainly be a lot wiser. This was by way of compensation for the time they spent away from their colony and in the wizard's company, reimbursing them for time lost.

However, after seven long and sometimes disappointing years as Raven's term as familiar came to an end, his health and temper had begun to suffer the effects of Silas' botched magic. He was now almost deaf in one ear, he had a slight limp in his front left leg and there was a smell of singed fur that simply refused to go away. In addition, he had developed a distinct hatred of grumpy wizards. Raven was looking forward to his retirement. Almost from the day Raven had arrived, at least as soon as he was aware of Ethan's impending retirement, he had begun counting down the days until he could return to his colony. It would be fair to say, that the returning Raven was a little disillusioned with the whole wizarding world by the end of *his* term as Silas' familiar.

As individual strands of cotton are drawn together and woven into a stronger, more resilient cord so are the lives of those at Highfell Croft and the many feral lives of the Greyfell Colony. The unbroken, seven-year cycle of familiar and mage, created a unique bond that reached back through the decades and as with any well-matched alliance, the union became greater than the sum of its individual parts.

At the time a new familiar leaves the colony to begin his term with the wizarding family, his chosen replacement would begin their training with the returning familiar and when seven years had passed, the exchange would be made again and the connection between colony and wizarding line, maintained. As Nightfire returned from the wizard's side to train Raven, Luna, who had been trained by Long-night, left the colony to take his place. Seven years later, when Luna returned, Raven took his place while he began training the next chosen one. It is to the birth of this lucky cat that we return and to a time just before Raven's seven difficult years began.

In a quiet corner of the moor, near to the blacksmith's croft, a proud queen prepared to give birth. Nightfire's sister, Leah, was one of three mothers whose kittens were to be considered for the role of familiar. She was Raven's mother and before the other cats had watched him leave for the wizard's croft and a new life of magic, she hoped to serve the colony by giving birth to another chosen one, and Luna's apprentice.

As Nightfire approached the end of his time as Raven's teacher, Leah gave birth to seven kittens. The first to arrive was a big strong tom, jet-black but for a small moon-shaped white patch on his chest. Next to come was a ginger tabby female followed by a tortoiseshell male and then a black and white male. Leah caught her breath during the pause in arrivals but all too soon, they began to come again. Another black and white, this time female and then a tabby tom after another well deserved pause, a near perfectly white kitten arrived, pure white but for four black socks. Leah hoped that this besocked kitten was the last but something felt wrong, there was still one more to come, but it was taking too long.

After a long wait, a seventh, tiny kitten finally arrived but Leah feared the worst when it lay still and did not move. She gathered them all together to keep them warm and began to wash them all carefully. When it came to the smallest, she gave it a special wash but it was so cold and tiny that Leah feared it was too late. It was at this point that Nightfire strolled over to investigate the new arrivals. As soon as he saw the tiny runt, he dashed onto the moors only to return moments later with a mouthful of leaves. He dropped the partly chewed leaves next to Leah and told her to lay the small kit on top of them. For a moment, nothing happened but then the kitten took a deep breath and let out a loud meow. Leah gathered-up the small bundle and brought it into the fold with its brothers and sisters.

'Thank you Nightfire, your quick thinking probably saved your young niece's life.'

'It was something Ethan showed me. As soon as I saw her, I remembered what to do. I guess the old wizard is still with us after all,' Nightfire replied. 'She'll be alright now but I doubt she'll ever be a fighter like her bigger brother!' Nightfire looked at the larger black male with the white sickle shaped scar on his chest. 'I think we might just have found Raven's replacement in this one.'

'That is for the elders to decide and besides, the other queens do not yet have their young, but I have to agree, he is a fine young tom.'

Leah returned to the task of nurturing her young but quietly she hoped that she could provide one more companion for the family to which they owed so much. Gradually the isolated, sheepless moor came alive with the sound of hungry kittens as the other queens in the colony gave birth to their litters.

Back then, as the new generation of Greyfell cats began its own story, Raven was already looking forward to beginning his with the wizarding family of Grimdyke. Seven years later and the situation had completely changed and he was now looking forward to drawing a line under his association with Greyfell. For almost the whole of his term at Greyfell, he had spent his time dodging flying potions, spitting out foul tasting herbs and generally trying to be somewhere else whenever Silas was looking for him.

Seven years ago, it had been so different. Then he had been excited and eager to begin but now it was the turn of one small black cat, known as Whitescar, who, just as Leah had hoped, had been chosen to be his replacement.

CHAPTER FOUR
Whitescar

Whitescar quickly grew and before long, he was almost twice as big as his brothers and sisters. Under his father's expert guidance, he quickly learned the skills of hunting. Between his mother and older brothers they taught him the art of concealment and how to stalk quietly, even when he was really too hungry to show patience. As the chosen one, Whitescar was apprentice to Luna but his progress had drawn the attention of the whole colony. They were all very fond of their new, would-be familiar and paid him far more attention than the other newcomers. All except for Nightfire. He had developed a special bond with a certain small black kitten, the niece he nearly lost.

She was an odd little thing, spending most of her time alone, either exploring the moors or staring across to the far-away hills from the roof of the forge. Something about her was different but Nightfire could not quite put his paw on exactly what it was. One day, as he stood guard over her while she played, he called Luna over to ask him what he thought. They both watched as she quietly amused herself, chasing the damselflies along the bank of the small beck. Luna agreed with Nightfire. There *was* something about her, something Ethan may have mentioned but the longer Luna was away from his old master, the less he remembered about his teachings. It had always been the way. When a retiring familiar had passed on his knowledge to his apprentice, he would forget all he had learned. Only then could he fully return to his feral cat life.

Once a spell or potion had been spoken of, it was forgotten as if it were a token, passed from one cat to another. Luna knew that if he talked about his time with Ethan to Nightfire, he would be unable to repeat it again to Whitescar. He had to return to his student but before he left, he did have one observation to make.

'This kit *is* different ... she does not charge around like her brothers and sisters. It's as if she considers all about her before acting. Maybe it's because she's smaller than them and yet I too sense something else in her ...'

Nightfire knew that Luna's duties were to encourage the new familiar in his charge and prepare him for Raven's return. This new and enigmatic little kitten was not really his concern. No, Luna needed to concentrate all his efforts on training Whitescar in preparation for his new role. Neither his own curiosity nor fanciful notions would change the way it had to be.

'No, this young kit isn't his task. She never was, she's mine,' Nightfire said resolutely.

He felt a responsibility for the kit whose life he saved and as her uncle, he would do all he could to help her ... but help her what?

'She's just a kit, Whitescar is the chosen one and yet ... Why *do* I always feel like there is an "and yet" when I look at her? I really need Ethan's help here.' Then something else occurred to him. 'Ethan? Ethan! I still remember him *and* my time at the croft ... that's definitely *not* the way it should be. I taught Raven all I knew, well, all he wanted to learn so why do I still remember every spell, every incantation and magical sign? Is it possible my work is not yet done?'

Despite his sudden confusion, Nightfire was clear about one thing. He sensed something strange about his young niece. It was as if she had a different path to follow, a special role to play but what it was, only time would reveal ... to both of them. Nightfire looked up again only to realise that the young kit had moved away and he was immediately concerned for her safety. It was a very large and dangerous moor for such a small kit to explore alone. First, he checked the area next to the forge before walking over to the brook that ran along the base of Greyfell Pike where he eventually caught up with her again.

'Hello, what are you doing so close to the water's edge?'

The kitten thought for a moment before replying.

'You're my uncle Nightfire, aren't you? My mum has told me all about you. *She* says that you've got special eyes.'

'Has she. You are still dangerously close to the stream. What is your given name, little one? What has Leah called you?'

'I don't have a name yet. Mum told me that you would choose it.' Nightfire was stunned. All this time and the kit did not have her given name. 'The others call me Fur-ball!'

'Brothers and sisters will tease.' Nightfire smiled. 'But that will not do at all, you must have a name and it must be the right one.'

As he spoke, Nightfire was becoming increasingly concerned by the kit's closeness to the edge of the riverbank but before he could call to her, she turned and jumped into the beck! Despite his natural hatred of water, Nightfire ran to the edge and was just about to jump in after her when she reappeared on the bank beside him carrying a small fish in her mouth.

'Well, that's something I've never seen before! Are you unharmed?'

'Yes, thank you uncle. I come here when I get hungry.'

'But the moors are full of food. There are mice and voles everywhere; the wizard Grimdyke has made it so.'

'I know, mum showed me. She even caught one for me but …'

'But?'

'But I *can't* eat it, not when it's talking to me!' his young niece protested.

Nightfire then remembered something else. Actually, he was able to remember *everything* his old master had taught him. Such thoughts normally only stayed with a familiar until they had trained the next familiar, unless …

'Ethan … he could talk with *me* but this, this is different,' and then he thought some more. 'What was Ethan up to?' Nightfire suspected his old master of setting in motion some greater plan but it was too early for him to make the pieces fit. He looked back to the kit as she sat waiting patiently. 'I can't keep calling you "Young-one" so I guess the first thing I must do is name you, as your mother suggests.' Nightfire considered a few proud family names from his past.

'Six-claws, Owl-eyes, Surefoot …' However, the real answer was right in front of him. 'We shall call you Becky, after the water you appear to love so much.'

'I'm Becky!' the young kit shouted as she chased round in a circle trying to catch another damselfly. 'Becky, Becky, Becky!'

'So tell me, Becky, what did you mean when you said your food talked to you?'

Becky suddenly stopped running then grew still and quiet.

'What's wrong? I only asked you what you meant.'

'The others laughed at me when I told them so I don't talk about it anymore and now I play by myself … or with the other animals.'

'Didn't Leah tell you that you shouldn't play with your food?'

'They're not my food, they're my friends. I knew you wouldn't understand.'

'No … I didn't at first but give me time, I think I may be getting there slowly. Come here and sit down next to me. Then you can tell me about your other friends.'

43

Becky then explained to Nightfire how she had first assumed that all creatures could talk to each other. She had been doing so from the time she was big enough to run onto the moor alone. She talked to the field mice about seed gathering and the water voles that lived in the banks of the beck. She even talked to the songbirds that filled the air with birdsong at the beginning and end of every day. Becky had wondered how they could remember such beautiful and complicated tunes. Then she stopped and looked at Nightfire.

'Why aren't you laughing, like the others?'

'Possibly because I'm a little older, maybe even a little wiser but most likely because a great friend of mine could talk with me the way you talk to your friends. Some nights we would just sit together and talk, sometimes we would chatter into the small hours of the morning.'

'What was he, a rabbit? They talk *very* fast!'

'No, this was a wizard friend, a very special wizard but one I am only now suspecting of being more devious than I first thought.'

'What's *beaverous* … something beavers do? Is it bad?'

'No *devious*, and in this case I think it might be very clever.'

Quite unexpectedly, Nightfire then found himself telling Becky all about Ethan and the time he had spent with the old wizard. It had nothing really to do with her but for some reason old memories began pouring out of him as if a tap had been turned on. As day turned into evening and then to night, the sky turned dark blue and speckled with stars and Becky continued to sit by her uncle's side, entranced as she listened to strange tales about a magical wizard called Ethan Grimdyke.

'Time to come back to the house now.'

It was Leah. She had left the two of them talking as long as she dared but now it was time for all the family to gather at the old forge. Night time was a time for hunting and foraging but for Becky it was time to talk with the older cats and learn from their great experience. The wisdom of years, Leah called it and their tales of strange places and equally strange beasts always enthralled the young kit. Becky thanked her uncle for the stories but most of all she thanked him for her new name. Then she bounded off after her mother.

'Becky, Becky, Becky!' she called excitedly as she ran.

'So, we are to call you Becky. It is a fine name and one I am sure others will learn of ... in time.' Leah smiled as they walked together back to the old abandoned smithy.

Nightfire sat quietly for a moment as he thought about what his young niece had said and what he had revealed to her. Then as the moor settled down for the night, he listened to the noises coming from the fell. It was faint but he could definitely hear chattering. It was also far too jumbled for him to make any sense of so Nightfire walked back to rejoin the colony. Why had he not noticed the chatter before, what else would he learn from his young niece? Nightfire's head was filled with questions but the biggest question on his mind as he returned to the others was ...

'What does it all mean?'

He could not help suspecting that the old wizard had set something in motion before he left his side.

'If only Ethan had thought to tell me what it was, I might have been able to help.'

As the days turned to weeks and weeks to months, Luna diligently passed on to Whitescar all he knew about being a good familiar. As he listened, Whitescar learned and with every tale of magic and adventure, the young tom grew more eager to join the wizard. Along with accounts of cured animals and retrieved valuables, Luna passed on detailed instructions on which herbs and flowers the wizard would need in his daily work. Whitescar would need to be able to recognise all of them and be able to find them on Barren Moor. As his training was restricted to Greyfell Moor, Whitescar would need to learn about the places the plants liked to grow. He needed to know at what time of year they flourished and which of the other plants might grow there to fool him. Luna explained how some plants had evil twins, look-alike plants that could confuse the unwary. Some of these doppelgangers could even kill, if mistakenly eaten instead of their beneficial counterpart. Luna showed Whitescar as many examples of these as he could find on the moor.

'As for the rest, you will need to use your sense of smell to guide you but never your sense of taste! That way leads to the long sleep.'

Whitescar looked shocked.

'I thought the old wizard was powerful. Can't he save me if I eat them?'

'Only if he is aware of your plight. If you are out on the moors when you eat the wrong plant, how will he know? And don't think that your strong legs will save you either. If you try to run back to the croft, the plant will kill all the faster. In such cases, your only chance is to eat grass ...'

'But that always makes me sick!'

'Yes and when it does you had better hope that you get rid of all the bad plant. Some of these green killers can be fatal even the smallest piece.'

'Then why are they there?'

'Everything has its purpose, Whitescar. It is not for us as familiars to understand all things. Master Ethan did say that used correctly, even some of the harmful ones had a good side but he warned me to stay away from them all the same. Now, on to the difficult part. Having probably put you off plants altogether, I am afraid there will be times when your master will ask you to fetch them for him. Whichever leaf, berry or flower is needed, you must collect it without harming the plant

… or yourself. You must carry them like a young kit in your mouth. To crush or even bruise them may cause you harm, it will certainly make them less useful to your master. This is why you must listen to all I say. These words may just save your life one day.'

'Right, don't eat the goods!'

'Eh? Oh yes, deliver everything intact, which brings me to what might be your greatest challenge. If you master tells you to collect a small shrew for him … what then?'

'I carry it as if it were a kit,' Whitescar repeated automatically.

'So when it is in your mouth and unharmed you will just carry it back to the croft?'

'Yes, carry it back …'

'Unharmed, despite the way it would taste?' Luna could see Whitescar's resolve beginning to weaken. 'A tasty morsel … right under your nose?' Whitescar started to drool at the thought.

'No, I would … wait a minute, you're doing this on purpose, aren't you?'

'Yes and for your own good. If you are asked to bring a creature back alive, that is the way it must be. Not slightly chewed, not with three legs but whole and unharmed!'

Whitescar thought for a while.

'Are you sure I'm the right one for this job? Only … I quite like voles and shrews and mice are ...'

'Look, I'll give you this piece of advice. Should you be sent on such an errand, fill your stomach before you leave. Eat from your bowl. The master will feed you while you are in his service; it is part of the arrangement. You must remember all that you have learned about hunting from your father but forget the kill.'

'Is it all going to be this difficult?'

'No, Whitescar, some things will be a *lot* harder!'

Luna and Whitescar then set out on a long tour of the moor and along the way, Luna showed his young apprentice where to look for all manner of healing plants, mosses and even some of the burrows where the more unusual creatures lived. Whitescar was starting to feel hungry so Luna did not dwell at the burrows for too long just in case the sight of a fat vole tested Whitescar's resolve before he was ready. From the banks of the beck, Luna took Scar, as he had begun calling him, to a small boggy area at the heart of the moor. The dark, torpid water bubbled gently and multicoloured domes began to appear on the surface.

'These soulless pools are very dangerous, Scar. There are hidden coils, deep within the water that can snare a cat's feet, while foul gasses draw life from the body of the unwary. Oh, they look harmless enough, but they taste of death and the water knots your stomach. Don't even think about trying to swim across them, use your head and instead walk around them.'

Whitescar stared deeply into the pool, looking for any signs of life.

'No newts, no frogs or fish ... no ... *blubble-blubb.*'

'Careful, what did I just tell you!' Luna pulled Whitescar from the water just as his head dipped below the surface of the stagnant brown liquor.

'I ... I felt like I was flying!'

'Drowning more like. I told you these were dangerous waters and what did you do ... you stuck your muzzle right up to it, right where the bubbles lurk, waiting to trap the foolish or inquisitive.'

'Sorry Luna.'

'Never mind "sorry" just let it be a lesson. There are things on the moor that have no form, no smell and cast no shadow and yet they can kill as swiftly as any hawk or buzzard.'

'What are *they*?'

'Oh, right, our moor here is protected, I forgot for the moment. That brings me to another danger. Greyfell Moor and all that lies between the pike over there and the ridge here, is under an enchantment cast by the first wizard to meet with our colony. Even though he is long gone, Ezra protects us still. This means, you will not have seen the flying death that is the buzzard and the hawk ... or the merlin, I nearly forgot that one. Even on Barren Moor they should not concern a tom of your size as they feed on smaller prey but I have seen them carry away a large rabbit ...'

'Do they steel our food too?'

'Yes, On Barren Moor I'm afraid so. On Barren Moor, there are *many* hunters, all after the same quarry. That is why the Grimdyke wizards have always looked after their familiars and food is given most generously at the croft. Enough talk of your stomach, you should remember to keep a watchful eye and ear open for these and the other hunters of that wild moor.'

'Other hunters?'

'Foxes, stoats the occasional weasel, otters sometimes, in the larger streams but they only hunt for fish, then there are ... but you need some surprises or life will be dull. Our protection ends at Highfell Ridge, the moor beyond is a most hostile place ... but cheer up, that's where you will be doing most of your hunting!' Luna laughed. Whitescar managed a weak smile.

'Where exactly am I going?' The question had been on Whitescar's lips for sometime now and he just had to know. Scar had heard much talk of the great wizarding family, of the long line of familiars that served them but no one ever said *where* it all took place.

'That is for Raven to reveal to you on his return. He will set the trail for you to follow. All you need to do is trace it back to Highfell Croft and without delay.'

'Without delay, right. So it's, get the scent and follow the trail.'

'Well, almost. I think Raven might appreciate it if you introduced yourself before taking the scent and dashing off into the night!'

'Right! So it's, "Hi" first, get the scent, follow the trail and then Highfell Croft … yes?'

'Near enough … for now. I hope the master has not run out of patience by the time you arrive,' Luna chuckled. 'He's going to need it.'

Day after day, Luna continued to teach Whitescar all about herbs, plants, tinctures and potions and then he made sure he knew all there was to know about the old skills.

'I assume your father, Darkstep, has taught you all about the old ways?'

'You mean about listening, looking and staying close to the ground?'

'Right. Now you do know that means more than just lying down on the job, don't you?'

'I *know*!' Whitescar replied indignantly, 'but it all sounded a bit far-fetched to me … listening to the sounds of nature, sniffing the air for change and seeing beyond what is visible … I thought he was kidding.'

Luna sighed. If there was one skill that a new familiar really needed at his side, it was a good grasp of the old-ways. Sadly they were not something easily taught, they could only be awoken in a young kit and later, talked about to a mature cat, by then it was too late to learn the skill.

'Tell me what you see,' Luna asked as he sank down onto the ground to await Scar's reply.

By this time, it was growing quite dark but a cat's eyes were far superior to most moorland dwellers and could still reveal a lot to the patient stalker.

'There's a frog just over the next rise …'

'Yes, but no points for detecting a noisy frog!'

Whitescar grumbled but then tried again.

'A hedgehog, in a hurry and away from his normal route …'

'Yes, another noisy visitor, anything else? Maybe something that hasn't announced its presence for all to hear.'

Whitescar narrowed his eyes at Luna. Luna ignored him and instead, allowed his own eyes to close as his senses reached out into the moors. The young tom then sniffed the air and following Luna's lead, Scar too closed his eyes.

'Food! … I mean a vole has just slipped into the stream from the far bank and a legless one stalks a small mouse along the bank top.'

'Better, much better. The legless one, as you put it, is Natrix, a grass coloured creature that likes to live near the bogs and ponds of the moor. They usually feed on live water food but this one must be really hungry to track a mouse … and before you start worrying, the protection spell makes sure they don't eat too many. This creature is harmless to us but you should not confuse it with its cousin, Vipera. They can be as long as your longest stretch and most short tempered and dangerous too, when surprised. You can easily identify Vipera by the zigzag warning along their backs, and their large blood-red eyes. They also compete for our food but they will eat almost anything they can get into their mouths! Don't worry; you are far too big to be swallowed!' Luna laughed but then immediately he grew serious again. 'No, it is their *bite* you should be wary of. Yes, they can look like a stick with a bad attitude but if you disturb one on Barren Moor and you are slow to retreat, their bite can kill, even the biggest cat. Be also warned, even when they appear to be dead they are to be avoided. They can be a most devious adversary so beware of the red eyes.'

'Right, avoid the devious sticks!' Whitescar replied.

'This is why you should be aware of *all* those around you at all times, not just the ones that taste good!'

'Ok, I'll try.'

'Try nothing! Be resolved and succeed! Failure could mean your death.'

'This job is beginning to sound a lot more dangerous than it looked in the advert.'

'Advert … what advert … Oh, I see… kits, *humph*! When you are in the company of your master, there will be few that are foolish enough to challenge you but you are not there yet, these creatures *are*. You will be trespassing onto their moor when you join Ethan so do not expect to be greeted warmly by them. Also you should remember that protection is a two way cat-flap …'

'Cat-who?'

'So, there are a few things you do not yet understand. You will understand when you reach the croft door. Now, where was I? Protection … the master will do all he can to protect you but it is your job to keep vermin away from the master's food store and herb collection. Potions need herbs and many other items besides. If they are eaten by vermin you will need to collect more so it is in your own interest to do a good job.'

'So eat the mice before they eat the greens?'

'No, they are not yours to eat.'

'What? The *master* eats them?'

'Inside the croft you will find a tall-sided jar. You must catch any … *trespassers* and collect them in the jar. The master will decide what happens to them after that.'

'What a waste!'

'Possibly but that's …'

'… Not for a familiar to say … yes, I know.'

'Good. In addition to the food … er, *pest* problem, you will have another duty of protection. While you serve the master, he will look after you and protect you against harm and you must do the same for him. The protection spell he will cast over you will add to your own natural skills and repay the years you spend with him. You must use your old-way skills to warn the master of unwelcome guests or the presence of another, whether they are human or magical creature. You must have faith in your protection and do all that you can to guard your master from all forms of spell, Bogle influence or curse that might be cast his way.'

'Curses? What, like *spit and fur balls*!'

'No, and mind your language. You may be the chosen one but there's no need for that. *Ticks and snagged-claws*, I mean, it's just not right for a familiar to use language like that.'

'No, but it's all right for you.'

'What … oh that, sorry, it just slipped out. Look, getting back to protection, what I meant was curses like malicious or harmful spells. It did not happen during my time with the wizard but tales of magical conflicts abound and not all magic is good like the magic of the Grimdyke line.'

'Right, so I'm to be a rat-catcher and bodyguard to a wizard with magical enemies.'

'If you are good at your job, yes, if not you will soon become a fond memory.'

'This just gets better all the time!'

'Not yet it doesn't … that is where the magic comes in.'

Luna then approached the difficult task of teaching Whitescar about incantations and spells. Though a cat could not use the same language as his master, it was still possible to cast some spells in felish, a cat's native tongue. These were limited to simple spells of self-defence, concealment, or debilitation, the latter being useful when a food bowl was empty and hunger gnawed distractingly at the mind. Within a few days Whitescar had mastered the basics of these advanced skills and as the end of his training approached, Luna was confident that he had taught Scar all he knew.

A new apprentice could never be too prepared but Luna felt that Whitescar had learned all he needed to know, at least to set him on the right road. The rest would be up to his willingness to learn from the wizard Grimdyke.

Nightfire found Becky a different proposition altogether. For every new skill he taught her, it seemed that she could teach him two. From her time spent with other creatures on the moors, Becky was already familiar with many herbs and grasses that flourished on the fell, in fact, many even Nightfire had not heard of. As he listened to her, it appeared that even the humblest of creatures had special knowledge of the fell. The birds knew which seeds were safe to eat, at least for them. The squirrels knew which of the nuts were most nutritious and how long they could store them. Becky even learned a little from the stoats and weasels, when they would talk and not try to trick her. Sometimes they would even brag to her about how they tracked and hunted for food. Becky told Nightfire how the stoats could attack and kill prey ten times their size. Sadly, her friends, the rabbits, appeared to be their favourite food. To make up for the rabbit's greater size and speed, a stoat or weasel would first mesmerise them with an energetic, almost balletic dance, before striking. Becky realised early on that this was one dance she should probably avoid watching. If they started their antics with her, she would walk away while the stoats were preoccupied, even though their tricks rarely worked on the creatures of Greyfell Moor.

Nightfire learned almost as much from his young charge as Becky did from him and soon their conversations turned to tales of magic and potions. Becky was a natural when it came to potions, tinctures and elixirs. These were powerful spells in liquid form and Becky took to them with ease. Before very long, Nightfire had moved on to the difficult art of spell casting in felish. In no time at all, Becky mastered the stunning spell, protection charm and cloak of inconsequence, a great spell for when a familiar needed to see but not *be* seen. It was at this point that Nightfire paused to consider his involvement with Becky.

'What am I doing? These skills are for a familiar not a … a …' Then he looked at his young niece and wondered. 'What are you, Becky, that you have me telling you all manner of things you should not know? How is it when I am with you I feel like I am training a chosen one again? I could be expelled from the colony for what I am doing! If only Master Ethan had given me a clue, a sign to show me what I should do.'

'You mean like this?'

Becky then disappeared into the banks of tall grass and heather and a few minutes later, she reappeared with something hanging around her neck.

'I found this in the large stone near to our home.'

Becky tipped her head and the chain slipped off to land at Nightfire's feet. He stretched out a paw and turned over the small medallion hanging from the chain.

'This belonged to old Master Ezra! I have seen pictures of him wearing it. Where did you find it?'

The pair then chased back to the forge but stopped short on the old track bed. Becky had led Nightfire to the very same boulder on which Ezra had sat as he awaited the decision of the Greyfell Colony all those years ago. Now, over a century later, Becky sat in Ezra's place on the rock. Nightfire joined her on the top of the boulder and waited for her explanation.

'It was right here, in this hole.'

Nightfire looked at the top of the stone where he could see a deep crack in the rock. He sniffed then extended one of his long arms deep into the cavity.

'It's too deep for me to reach the bottom. How on earth did you get the chain out?'

'When I saw it shining in the rock I tried to reach it too but I couldn't. Then I remembered my friends. I asked a mouse to pull it out for me.'

'A mouse? You used your food to get Master Ezra's talisman out of the rock?'

'The mouse wasn't my food!' Becky protested strongly. 'But it did take a long time before he would let me carry him to the rock.'

'How on earth did you persuade a mouse to let you pick it up in your mouth?'

'I gave him my word I wouldn't eat him!'

'It appears that your word carries much weight for one so small.'

Becky then told Nightfire how she had explained to her small accomplice what she wanted him to do. She told him that she had found something that sparkled deep inside the stone. The mouse eventually agreed that as reward for not eating his kind, he would help her to retrieve the sparkler. Once again, Becky had carefully lifted the mouse onto the rock where she had shown him the deep hole and the sparkler hidden inside.

'Murry didn't mind. He said he liked deep burrows and small holes.'

'Murry?' Nightfire replied curiously.

'Yes, Murry. Everyone should have a name. Anyway, the hardest part was hiding Murry from the others or he would have been a snack for them, instead of my friend. Anyway, Murry dragged the chain back out of the hole for me. He said it was too heavy at the other end because there was something attached to it. Eventually, as he dragged the chain out, I could reach it with my paw and so I pulled Murry out along with the chain.'

'So, without the help of your foo … er, *Murry*, you would not have been able to retrieve it?'

'Friends help each other, it's what they do.'

56

'It appears we still have much to learn from each other.'

'*Anyway* …' Becky did not like having her story continually interrupted, even by Nightfire. 'Then I hid the chain on the moors in an empty burrow that Murry found for me. So, is it important, the chain thing, only I like wearing it when I'm alone on the moor, it makes me feel safe and not so alone.'

'Well I guess that answers my question. You have found your connection to Ezra and I have my sign. Where this will lead us, only Ethan knows but it means that we still have much work to do, you and I, and a lot to teach each other over the coming months. Also, for now at least, I think the less the others know about this the better, until we know where it is leading us.'

With most of the colony's attention firmly focussed on Whitescar and his training, Nightfire and Becky's strange schooling sessions went largely unnoticed, although Leah had her suspicions.

CHAPTER FIVE
Raven's Return

As Raven's last year with the wizard Grimdyke drew to a close, eager anticipation gripped the colony as the time grew near for the retiring familiar to return and his replacement to begin his own long journey of discovery. Although the colony felt enthusiastic, their feelings were not shared by Raven, unless he was thinking about his own retirement. Seven years earlier, although somewhat battle scarred and weary, Nightfire's only regret as he faced leaving Highfell Croft was that he would miss his old master and the adventures they had shared. It was true that Nightfire had some fading scars and a few patches of fur that were slow to re-grow but he would not have missed a minute of his time with Ethan. Raven's master however, was the younger and totally inexperienced, Silas Grimdyke, and unlike his father, Silas would not be putting right his familiar's minor wounds and scars before sending him back to the colony. He had no idea how to.

After one final spell from Ethan, Nightfire had departed in the best of health. He had been restored to the fitness of youth and his journey home was spent in pleasant reflection as he thought back over the past seven busy years. In contrast, when it came Raven's time to return to his colony, he would be forced to limp home with his singed fur a constant reminder of Silas' botched attempts at spell-casting. As retirement approached, Raven had only one thing on his mind and that was, getting away with at least *some* of his nine lives still intact.

'Take it one day at a time, Raven. First, get through the next night, just one more night!' Raven muttered bitterly as he hobbled around the kitchen, skulking from chair to chair in an attempt to stay out of Silas' direct line of fire.

'What are you grumbling and growling at, cat? The only thing you have brought this household is misery and fleas!'

Raven knew *exactly* where the fleas had come from and it was not from him. He suspected that the master himself had brought most of them in from some poor animal he had failed to rid of them. Silas would still dabble in magic from time to time but his heart was never in it and so the spells naturally failed. Real spells came from the heart and out of an unselfish desire to do good. With every failure of good magic, Silas' interest in the darker forms of wizardry grew. It had all started with his banishing of the villagers. Although their staying away was not a direct result of magic, even so it gave him the much-needed confidence to try again, unfortunately in the same dark manner. Silas could now reduce objects to dust with a flick of his wand, whither plants or pick off flies by exploding them one by one, as they flew around the oil lamps at night. He could also stun wildlife, a trick he frequently used to fill the cooking pot but thanks to his speed, Raven had never been on the receiving end of one of Silas' full stun charms, although the occasional lucky shot would give him a dead-leg for a few hours. Raven's sheer grit and determination to endure, and his desire to uphold his cat family name, was responsible for him staying the course. Many times, he had left the croft in the dead of night, determined to return to the colony and face the disappointment of his family, only to go back to Silas when his nerve returned. There were times when it felt like the shameful, quiet life of an outcast, would be a good trade, compared with all the aggravation Silas had caused him over the years. What would a few jibes and snide remarks behind his back be, when compared with fireballs thrown at his tail or the times Silas had tried to turn him into a dog.

'A dog, I ask you! I'd rather be a human! No, on second thoughts, I'd better just keep dodging the spells. I really don't fancy being either much.'

Many times, over the past seven long years, Silas had returned to the pile of peat blocks by the hearth and repeated the same incantation. Every time the result was the same, no new shiny gold, just a slight smoky whiff and a lot of cursing from Silas. Unfortunately for Raven, Silas was eventually able to turn the pitchers of water into beer … well, something that smelled more like fermented bog-water. For seven long years, as the villagers stayed away, only the more inquisitive children ever approached the croft but luckily for Raven, they usually brought much needed food for him. The children had realised that unlike Silas, Raven was really quite friendly and intelligent too. As a result, when they saw how thin he was becoming, they brought kitchen scraps from home for him. The children were really all Raven had to lighten his days but the nights were a different matter altogether.

In his sleep, Silas would mutter constantly, his troubled mind replaying the events of the day. Sometimes he would even mutter incantations or spells. The first Raven was aware of this dangerous habit was when his favourite chair vanished from beneath him as he slept one night. From that moment on, Raven could hardly relax at all as darkness fell. The best he could do was to rest with one eye open and one ear pricked, constantly on the lookout for trouble and usually finding it.

'Mum-fibble … Eri-dibble … Er … Era … ERADICO!'

Silas would shout in his sleep and another vase, chair or lamp would explode into smoke. When morning came and Silas awoke, he would forget he had ever cast the spells, which fortunately would restore the missing items to their former condition. Raven did not relish the thought of testing whether *he* would be restored alongside the ornaments if he were ever accidentally exploded. Wisely, he decided not to put it to the test, his master might just prefer the solitude and leave him as smoke to blow away in the morning breeze. Of all the sleep-cast spells Silas could mutter, the most alarming was when the opposite would happen and instead of evaporating an object, a new one would appear. One such night, Silas began to dream and as he dreamed, he mumbled.

'Ermine ... for me, Prince Fudgebucket ... that *would* be nice, two lumps please ... erf ... esk ... EXSISTO!'

When this spell escaped into the night so too did all manner of strange creatures from his dreams. With no thought of form behind the spell, almost anything could appear. Raven even thought he saw a three-headed dog appear one night but he did not wait around to find out. These strange creation spells were almost the exact opposite of the eradico spell. When cast, the smoke that had gathered in the room during the night would suddenly condense to form whatever Silas was thinking about in his bizarre dream and Silas could have some *very* strange dreams. Many such unforgettable night visitors followed as Silas went on to create snakes, small dragons, elves, bats and even bars of gold. If Silas had only known about his temporary wealth but as usual, when he awoke, all that was left of his creations would be a pawl of smoke that hung in the air as all the objects vanished again.

Possibly Raven's most terrifying night followed a particularly damp and cold day. During the day, strong winds had rattled the croft windows while rain dripped steadily through the slate roof. Silas had been trying to start a fire in the hearth but with no success. The peat was damp and the kindling he had left outside in the rain. Silas tried all kinds of hokum to start the fire. In fact, he used *any* words that came to mind that sounded anything like fire.

'FLAMMO! … Oh, what's another good one? INFLAMMATION! No, no, not that, I'm rather glad that one failed! INFLAGRANTE oh no wait, that means something *altogether* different. What *was* it Ethan used to get this thing started?'

'Actually, it was usually some of the paraffin from the oil lamps, but as you forgot to buy any, you might as well keep shouting at the logs!' Raven was most unimpressed with Silas' performance so grumbling under his breath, in very basic felish, he left Silas for the warmth and comfort of his sleeping box in the kitchen.

It was during the night however, that the trouble really started. In an effort to keep warm, Silas went to bed early only to find he was even colder under the damp covers than before. As a result, he shivered for most of the night, until the moment he started talking in his sleep again.

'Polar bear selling peppermints? Not today thank you. Koala bears selling cola, no thanks! Dung-beetles? Well whatever you're selling I *definitely* don't want any!' Then he started to ramble, which was always bad news for Raven. 'Dung-dong … Ung-ing … ig-ig … IGNIS!'

'Oh trust him to get it right now!' Raven muttered from inside his warm cardboard box. 'He's had all day to get a fire started and now he thinks of the right spell.'

Raven then realised that it had actually begun to get warmer, in fact, a little too warm for his liking. He poked a weary head over the lip of the box only to discover that the croft was well alight. He yowled. Despite his dislike for his master, this would not be a fitting end … for either of them. He yowled again, even louder this time but the smoke was already making him cough. His plan was to wake Silas but the only water spell he knew was not powerful enough and the small jet he could produce evaporated in the heat long before it ever reached Silas' face. Raven hurriedly tried a few more spells but the thick choking smoke and the leaping flames were making it difficult to concentrate. By this time, all exit routes out of the croft were well alight and they were both trapped! Raven was now afraid that he would not survive to enjoy his retirement.

Flames rapidly began to spread across the floor where they started to lick at the linen on Silas' bed. Just then, a small spark from the burning furniture landed on the end of Silas' nose and he awoke with a start. In an instant, the flames were all gone, the furniture and belongings restored and the heat quenched. All that remained to tell the tale was a small fire in the hearth and a slightly singed and very annoyed looking cat.

'So he'll restore this place and leave me smouldering! After all I've done for him ... typical!' Raven climbed back into his box, hissed and then spat at his tail in an attempt to put out the last patch of smouldering fur.

'Brains, Raven, use your brains, even if *he* can't! AQUA-PROFUNDO! Drat, that's too much. Now I'll have to sleep on the chair again. *Snagged-claws*, how I hate wet fur!' Raven muttered miserably as he retreated to the cushion on the large rocking chair and some well-earned sleep.

As he slept, Raven had an unusually pleasant dream. He dreamt that he was in the service of a great and powerful wizard, one totally unlike Silas. In the dream, his master had called together all his familiars and staff for a crisis meeting.

'I'm sorry my dear friends but my time with you is coming to an end and I must move on. I have written to other members of the wizarding community and they are willing to offer jobs to you all, er, all except for Raven. I am afraid that you will be returning to your colony.'

'Why? I served you well, why is there no position for me?' Raven mumbled in his sleep.

'You are not to be sacked dear friend, just … *relocated*,' the grand wizard explained. 'I still have use for you and it is very important that you …'

'SNORT!' Silas stirred, woken by Raven's mumblings as he slept. 'Wassup? Who's there … what the? Oh it's you, you flea bitten old failure!' Silas threw an old boot at Raven.

Luckily, the heavy boot missed him; *unfortunately,* it hit the rocker's curved bottom rail, which catapulted Raven out of the chair. The force sent him flying across the room and out of his puzzling dream.

'Important that I what? Eh, what's happening?'

'Now that you're up, you can make an early start on replenishing the potions cupboard,' Silas snapped at the half awake and still bewildered cat. 'Take a look at the jars. We're out of nearly everything! Go on and don't come back until you have them all.'

'But I had an important mission!' Raven thought. 'If I only knew what it was.'

Still sore and singed from the effects of the fire, Raven did as he was told. He climbed onto the nearest chair to the cupboard and pulled the door open. Silas was right, nearly all the jars were empty.

'Wolfsbane, Monkshood, Feverfew, Valerian … this will take me all day … what am I thinking, make that all week!'

Raven then noticed something else. Pinned to the inside of the potions cupboard door was a dingy calendar. Each day Raven would check the ingredients and mark off one day on the chart but today's date was ringed with fine scratches. He had carefully scratched around this most important date with his claws.

'It's today!' Raven said in disbelief, 'It's … *today*! I'm finally … free.'

Today was the day, before the seventh night, of the seventh month, of the seventh year and Raven's time as familiar had at last come to an end.

'I can go home!' He still could not believe it. 'All I have to do is get back to the colony and then I can relax again.'

For the first time in ages Raven could now smell something other than burning fur in his nostrils; he could smell freedom. He jumped smartly down from the shelves of the potions cupboard and headed for the cat flap in the back door.

'*Now* you show some enthusiasm, finally a bit of pride in your work!' Silas called sarcastically after Raven as he headed for home.

'Raven was just about to leave through the flap for the last time when he noticed Silas' boots sitting by the back door.

'Maybe just one last trick, a parting gift for Silas.'

Raven busied himself with the old boots for a few moments before heading for the door again. 'That will be a nice little surprise for him when he puts his boots on … and I didn't even need to used magic!'

Raven then paused with one paw resting against the swinging flap.

'It was only a dream so why has it got me so frustrated and why is the fur on the back of my neck standing on end? He said, "It is very important that I" … that I what? The dream was too real to be *just* a dream but what could it all mean? I'm free of Silas now so it can't be about him … The old wizard was wearing a talisman but it was not one of Silas' so where have I seen it before. This is most irritating, like a fleabite that's in need of a good scratch.'

Raven then slipped quietly out of the croft and savoured his first deep breath of freedom. Then he remembered that he still had work to do. His last duty would be to lay the trail for his replacement to follow.

'My replacement! Boy is *he* in for a shock when I tell him that Ethan has gone and that the idiot son is in charge. Ah well, he will be young and strong and if Luna has taught him well, he should be all right. At least he will be starting with a full coat of fur!'

Raven stopped again by the garden gate, jumped onto the drystone wall and took a last look over Barren Moor.

'Well, the adders and foxes will need to find someone else to chase from now on but at least they kept a fellow on his toes.'

Raven turned his back on the moor and headed for the bleached limestone escarpment of Highfell Ridge. Retracing his steps from seven years earlier, he followed a small footpath towards the base of the towering ridge. Hidden from view, unless one knew exactly where to look, was a narrow cleft in the hillside and this little known track was the only safe way to pass through the high ridge.

With the advantage of an early start and an eagerness to return to his colony, Raven set off on the long trek home. However, the words from his dream did not fade away as he expected, instead they stayed with him as he began his journey.

'Important that I … what? And that talisman … I'm sure it's important too …'

Raven started the long steady climb into the deep hillside cleft. Walls of sheer limestone soon began to tower high above him as he travelled and although it was still daylight, the slender ravine was so deep that it even caused the light around him to grow dim. The gloom was no match for Raven's acute night-vision and he strode on confidently towards Greyfell and the colony he missed so much. His stride then quickened as he recalled the old forge and blacksmith's croft. Almost an hour later and still deep within the hillside, Raven was nearing a very important point in his journey.

Cascading down from the hill high above, was a small waterfall, which splished, splashed and trickled its way down to the trackway where he stood. The water was cool, sweet and very welcome to a thirsty traveller. Raven knew the area well and not all the water that ran or collected there was fit to drink. Even this sweet refreshing stream would soon disappear underground to mingle with the waters of the mine, after which it became tainted and filled with dissolved metal ores. On the far side of Highfell Ridge, old mine workings brought the water to the surface again where it ran from the open mouths of mine levels to pollute the moorland streams, pools and becks. All creatures of Greyfell Moor knew of the bad water and avoided any contact with it. Few animals had tasted the water's metallic tang of death and survived and those that had were never quite the same again.

Raven was now halfway through the hillside but he still had many miles to go. He set off again and after a few more minutes, the pathway in the narrow rift changed and the ground beneath his paws began to fall away again. In another hour, he would see the familiar sight of Greyfell Moor and if Silas had not damaged his sight too much, he would get his first, distant glimpse of the old forge. Urged on by the slight downwards gradient, Raven began to trot. He was like a young kit again and the call of home and family beckoned strongly. A slight breeze was picking up in the ravine and he could smell the peaty waters of the moor beyond its confining walls. Two more bends and one long straight run and he would be out.

'Around this next bend ...'

As the sun met his gaze, he struggled to see clearly in the bright sunlight. At last, Raven could see the moor, *his* moor. Soon there would be no more predators, no adders, or weasels stealing his next meal, just an endless supply of food and the good company of family and friends. Raven's eyes quickly adjusted to the brightness and on the far side of the moor, a few miles along the valley, he could just make out the outline of the smithy that was home to the Greyfell Colony. Raven sat for a few minutes just to take in the view. It was the first time in seven years that he had something to which he could look forward.

'I wonder how my old mentor, Nightfire, is doing. Enjoying retirement, I shouldn't wonder and what of my replacement. I hope Luna has taught him well. I hope he is a tough and resourceful tom. He will be facing a most difficult time ahead and he will need all the edge Luna can give him. Now it's most important I should scent the approach to the ravine. Without this, the new familiar would face an impossible journey over the top of Highfell Ridge.'

Raven then descended onto the moor where he felt instantly at home. The minute he emerged from the ravine, he could sense Ezra's protection charm. It covered the valley like an invisible umbrella. After all these years, the colony remained safe from predators and so too did their food. As long as there was a Grimdyke wizard at Highfell Croft, Ezra's enchantment would continue to protect them.

'As long as there is a wizard ...' Raven thought. 'Does Silas even qualify as a wizard? He knows few if any spells that work well and has almost no knowledge of potions. This is not good. Why wouldn't he listen to me? Why did he insist on using dark magic when good was stronger. I must warn my replacement. The future of the great wizarding line of Grimdyke may well rest in his paws and with it, the future of our whole colony.'

Raven quickened his step as he began to pick his way across the wide moor to the beck that ran at the far side and in the shadow of Greyfell Pike. He carefully wound his way past banks of heather, by damp beds of reed and around the deep black ponds and bogs. Raven carefully scented the safest route for his replacement to follow, hoping that whoever it was, he was an exceptional cat and up to the task of turning Silas back to good magic. After many hours of travel and the onerous task of scenting the trail, Raven was running on empty. He needed food but most of all he needed to drink.

'Somewhere around here is a small spring, now where is it?'

It lay somewhere off the track home but Raven knew it was not far away, if he could only find it. Suddenly, as he made his way through the coarse undergrowth, Raven found his way barred by a large expanse of very dark water. A few flies hovered aimlessly above its still surface and a handful of frail looking water boatmen scudded across the scummy liquor, but apart from them and the odd water strider, the pond appeared to be void of life. This clearly was not the safe, sweet drink he sought but Raven had been unable to locate the spring and he now had a desperate thirst.

'Maybe just one small sip, there can't be any harm in that.'

He bent down to sniff the water. It smelled of death and decay but he was so thirsty.

'Just one ...'

A sudden splash of cold water then brought him to his senses. He had breathed in the foul and dangerous gases that bubbled up from the bottom of the bog and in two seconds, they had overpowered him and as Raven slipped into unconsciousness, his head had dipped into the water. Raven shook himself dry, being careful not to lick any of the water from his fur.

'That was too close! What was I thinking ... I *wasn't* thinking! I must be slipping, that was a rookie mistake.'

As soon as his head was clear again, Raven's thoughts returned to the matter of the fresh-water spring. 'Think Raven, use the old ways.'

He then settled down on a small hummock of coarse grass to do just that. Pushing all thoughts of hunger and thirst from his mind, he listened to the sounds the moor was making all around him.

'Right, that's better. Now what have we got ... the wind is making the reed beds rustle ... the sun is cracking the seedpods of a nearby plant ...' Raven sniffed at the breeze, 'and somewhere down wind is ... sweet-water! I can smell it, and in the small pool where the water surfaces, a bird is taking a bath. Ah, food *and* drink!'

Raven stalked and slinked his way towards the spring, following the sweet smell of fresh water and the promise of a long-overdue meal.

Half an hour later, when he had satisfied his needs, his mind returned to the business of finding his colony. Scenting and searching, he retraced his steps from seven years earlier as if he walked this way only yesterday. The sun was warm, the grasses smelled fresh and as his homing instincts went on automatic, his mind found time to wander.

'I guess I'll have to get used to finding my own food again. Still, if I ever find another clothes peg, I can always try the chicken dipper spell again! I wonder how long the magic will stay with me after I return. I'm going to miss the food that the children of the village used to bring. I'm going to miss having a full food bowl! "Cold-cuts" yes, I think that's what they called them. I wonder where they nest. Which part of the moors do "cold-cuts" call their own? They must roam somewhere nearby.'

Then he remembered his peculiar dream and the old wizard's wish that he should complete an important task.

'I wonder if Nightfire can shed any light on my dream. I wonder if he still remembers his time at Highfell ... no, what am I thinking, once spoken, forever lost, that is the way. Yet, he was always a bright tom so maybe he can still help me.'

Raven pressed on and doubled his step as some of his youthful agility began to return with thoughts of home. Within a short hour or two, he encountered the first of the colony's lookouts.

'Stop, come no nearer this land belongs to Greyfell Colony. Identify yourself stranger!'

'Ringtail … is that you? I would hardly have recognised you. A sentry now, well done.'

'Raven? Raven you old moggie, how's your ticks and fleas? It's great to see you again.'

'Well the ticks have gone and I swapped my fleas for some that Silas brought home but it's the singed fur that gets me down. The smell just doesn't go away.'

'The other boundary guards will meet us soon. They are all around the camp tonight to make sure we didn't miss your arrival.' Ringtail rubbed alongside Raven as they walked back to the smithy, after all, seven years was a long time to be away from a brother. 'It's really great to have you back!'

'I'm sorry to say this, and don't take it the wrong way, but I'm really glad to be back!' Raven sighed, now that the worst was behind him.

As they walked, he and Ringtail talked about his time with Silas, and how much the old wizarding family had changed. Raven also warned Ringtail that it could all be over soon, the family line, their colony's protection, everything. As Raven solemnly explained,

'How is a dolt like Silas ever going to attract a mate? No, I'm afraid I foresee dark times ahead, very dark times, especially for the next familiar … well, for the entire Greyfell Colony!'

Ringtail assured Raven that his replacement would be more than up to the task. He was a giant of a cat, a strong tom as black as jet and bearing the white sign of the new moon.

'He's called Whitescar, one of Leah's brood,' Ringtail announced with pride. 'And our younger brother.'

'I have to warn him … oh, hold on a minute, almost forgot to mark that turn, right, where was I?'

'Worrying the fur-balls out of me! That's where.'

'If Whitescar is strong and determined, I'm sure he'll be fine but he'll need to be one terrific familiar to conjure a mate for Silas!'

The two cats laughed but as the seriousness of their situation sank in Ringtail began to wonder what they should do next.

'Are you *sure* about warning Whitescar?'

'All the way across the moor I was determined to warn him, even after I'd been confoggated by the marsh gas, I was going to warn him … but now, what could I say? I don't want to put him off. After all, he *has* to go, despite Silas being what he is.'

'And what's that, Raven?'

'A complete and utter dog!'

'Whoa … as bad as that?'

'Worse! He's almost completely non-magical and he's bitter with it. His best spells he casts in his sleep! That reminds me, I must warn Whitescar about the sleep-casts if nothing else, and make sure he knows the aqua-profundo spell. Whitescar may be our only hope of turning Silas back to the good side but he will need to stay on his toes.'

As they neared the forge, more guard cats joined them on their walk home and soon Raven and Ringtail were accompanied by a small crowd of inquisitive friends. Around the next bend in the river then over the old disused track-bed and they were home. The last surge of cats then rushed forward from the old buildings to greet the retiring familiar, all that is except for the nursing mothers who were making sure their kits had a head start on being the next familiar after Whitescar.

Suddenly, from out of the crowd rushed a large black form. It bulldozed its way through the throng of cats, knocking them aside as it made its way directly towards where Raven was standing with Ringtail. The last few cats parted and Raven was hit by the runaway mountain of black fur.

'Hi, I'm Whitescar,' he shouted in a rush, 'Now get the scent, then it's follow the trail to Highfell Croft! ... Bye! ... See you all in seven years ... don't wait up!' and he was gone.

Luna stepped forward into the gap created by Whitescar's departure.

'Welcome home Raven. Yes, that blur was your replacement, Whitescar. A stronger, quicker and fitter tom I have yet to see. He is also eager, enthusiastic ... and impatient!'

Raven looked down the path as Whitescar raced after the scent trail that would lead him across the moor to Highfell Croft.

'But I didn't even get an opportunity to wish him good luck! I didn't get to say *any* of the things I had planned!'

By this time, Nightfire had joined Luna and Raven.

'It's good to see you Raven, well most of you. You seem a little threadbare.'

'That's part of what I needed to warn Whitescar about.'

As friends and families welcomed Raven back into the colony, he explained about the worsening situation at Greyfell.

'Ethan has left the croft.'

'The old master wouldn't just leave!' a panicked tabby female replied.

'I hadn't been there for five minutes when he handed Silas the keys and left.'

'So there is a new wizard in place,' a large tortoiseshell tom replied with authority.

'Not exactly ... there's a *Silas* in place but he's no wizard.'

73

Muttering and murmuring spread around the group like wildfire. Some cats dismissed the talk as "fear mongering" while others even considered leaving the fell at first light. Luna climbed onto a large rock and tried to sound the voice of reason.

'Whitescar is strong. He is the chosen-one. He learned everything I taught him quickly and thoroughly ... *well most of it* ... We must put our faith in Whitescar and the strong wizarding line of Greyfell.'

This appeared to settle most of the debate and the crowd began to break up and return to their homes. Old friends of Raven rubbed shoulders with him before they left and told him they wanted to hear all about his exploits the first opportunity he had. Small kits and young eager cats were already drawing lots to see who would join the group for the first round of tales of Greyfell Croft and the wizard Grimdyke.

'I have a feeling in my tail that won't go away, I ...' Raven sighed to Luna and Nightfire.

'When you can get away from the kits and your other fans, I have something I wish to discuss with you, Raven, *before* you begin your time with the next familiar,' Nightfire suggested.

'If there is a next,' Raven replied quietly so that the others would not hear.

'Give Whitescar a chance. He is strong and fearless ... he'll come through for us, just you wait and see,' Luna replied with a slightly unconvincing note of confidence.

Nightfire smiled sympathetically.

'Luna, I'm sure you did a great job with his training. He's been given the best start any familiar could wish for. What I wanted to talk about concerns something strange that has happened here during Raven's absence.'

'Ah, you mean the misfit.'

'And as far as the next generation of familiar is concerned, the smart money is on Nappa as being the next apprentice,' Nightfire replied to Raven's growing concerns. 'If she can stay awake long enough for you to train her that is!'

'A female ... just what I need, another challenge!' Raven laughed.

CHAPTER SIX
Journey into Darkness

As the colony settled down for the night to swap tales and speculate about the wizard Silas, Whitescar continued on his long and difficult journey to Highfell, unaware of their growing concerns or the problems that lay ahead for him. In the night, the once familiar moors would show the intrepid traveller a new face, one lined with mystery and danger. The bright pools of fresh water in daylight became dark traps that could swallow a hasty cat, whole, leaving no evidence of their terrible fate for those that remained. The stubby trees would twist into unspeakable evil forms and cast shadows of doubt even on the most determined traveller. While the keen hunting eyes of an experienced cat were more than a match for the darkness, colours and sounds would change as strange smells and shadows distorted the truth. The only companions a nocturnal explorer could rely on were a steady nerve and the wisdom of years. However, the latter was hardly to be found in abundance with the young Whitescar.

A replacement familiar needed to be a master of many skills but most of all he needed to be young and fit. His term with the wizard would be long and arduous and only the fittest would survive. Their training with the colony left little time for talk of "the old days", little time for reminiscing with the older cats of the group and sharing their knowledge. If it had, maybe Whitescar could have been better prepared. However, as the older cats reminded him, "ifs and buts catch no mice", and this was the way it *had* to be, the way it had *always* been, which left Whitescar to rely on Luna's teachings and on his own wits for his survival.

'I don't remember the beck being this noisy before … come on, concentrate Scar, this is what you trained for. What was that? Only a vole, get a grip … now where's the next turn?'

Whitescar had reached the point along the stream where he had to leave the banks of the beck and cut across the broad expanse that was Greyfell Moor but at least with Ezra's enchantment in place, he did not need to worry about the *flying death*. He had heard stories of large owls, driven to attack anything that moved in the night, their hunger blinding them to the size of their prey. No cat from the colony had ever been carried off by the "Big-eyes" but a few bore reminders of their encounter. They carried deep, piercing scars that cut deep into their backs, lasting reminders that made walking a forever-pain for them. Whitescar shook himself as if trying to shake off the spectre of fear.

The path across the moor now began to weave in and out of deep banks of heather and across spongy, springy beds of sphagnum moss that squelched and squirted uncomfortably between his toes.

'Why are the hours of darkness always longer than the hours of daylight? Why are leaps and bounds shorter, while miles are so much longer … and why have I started talking to myself?'

The night was beginning to weave its spell on the young traveller and if he were not strong, doubt would make its home in his thoughts.

'Why did Raven pass this way? It's as if he's tracking a wind-devil. I'm sure he's going in circles! Great, I guess that means I am too!'

Whitescar wound round and around, unknowingly following Raven's meanderings after his encounter with marsh gas and his mind-numbing confoggation until eventually, he found the reason for Raven's strange behaviour.

'Not a death bog! What was he thinking?' Whitescar could not imagine what could have driven Raven to stop at such a place. 'Surely he didn't drink the water. Well *I'm* not making the same mistake! This is no fit place to rest.'

Whitescar quickly located the trail again and turned to leave just as a large bubble of gas ignited behind him in the bog, illuminating the eerie scene with its pale yellow glow. Whitescar doubled his stride and headed for the towering ridge but Raven's wanderings before he encountered the bog were even more haphazard than after and now led Scar on another difficult and winding trail.

'Raven must have been desperate to drink there. Only great thirst could have done this to him.'

He sniffed and tracked, running along the straighter stretches but taking his time when the way became difficult to follow. Time slipped by but eventually, Whitescar reached the drier fringes of the moor and by now, he was able to appreciate how Raven must have felt.

'I could really do with a nice clear stream right now, fresh, sweet bubbling water … snap out of it Scar, you still have miles to go yet and the wizard must not be kept waiting. I can't be the first familiar to delay his great works or leave him unprotected.'

Whitescar tried to forget the growing thirst he felt inside and concentrate instead on the trail and for a while, it worked. In the gloom as he walked, Whitescar noticed a change underfoot. The soft carpet of grass, moss and reed was now liberally sprinkled with small stones. The stones were hard to avoid and rough on his paws but he kept going. Within minutes, he began to feel that there were now more stones than grass and at that moment, the moor gave way completely to the jumble of stones that was a landslide of small boulders and shingle. This carpet of loose scree was where the trail led and that was where he had to go. The bleached white surface of the stones only reminded Whitescar of how thirsty he had become and once the thought had taken root, it was all he could think of.

'It must be close now and whatever happens, I have to go through with it, it will be worth it to become the great wizard's next familiar. Besides, I am sure that anything that might happen to me he can easily put right with a simple spell or potion.'

Whitescar looked up to see the moonlight reflected in the towering rocks of Highfell Ridge and he wondered how he was ever going to get to the top, never mind down the other side again. The dry limestone scree was making following the trail difficult and it was as if the rocks themselves could neutralise the scent trail, making it nearly impossible to follow. He was sure it led to the large mushroom shaped rock but where it led from there was a mystery. Whitescar wandered around the large boulder, sniffing as he went. After his second time around, he was beginning to give up hope but then he thought about his situation again.

'It *has* to be here somewhere. Raven wouldn't just leave me here to climb the peak on my own, without a trail to follow.'

His mouth was dry and so too was his nose and Whitescar realised that his senses were being dulled by his growing thirst. Still mindful of the passing hours and not wishing to delay any longer than he was forced to, he headed back to the edge of the moor where he hoped to find some dew on the grass and reeds. Minutes later, after nuzzling, sniffing and licking around some of the hollows, he had found enough moisture to wet his nose and mouth and even a drop or two to drink. Slightly more refreshed, he headed back to the mushroom stone.

'Right, come on Scar, if you fail this test you don't deserve to be familiar to Grimdyke. Concentrate … take in the sounds of the moor. Deep breath and a clear head, then start again. What have we here … rabbit and over here, a mouse … *fhew*! They *really* know how to lay a trail. Now what's this, *urgh* ants! They're nearly as bad as fleas. Over here then … more rabbits, a weasel and … Raven!'

Whitescar was back on the right trail again and he bounded off up the blanket of loose stones, sniffing as he ran. The trail appeared to lead to the base of a sheer cliff and he was just beginning to wonder how on earth he was ever going to scale it, when he felt a breeze in his whiskers. The air was cooler than the breezes coming off the moor, with a hint of water in its stony, earthy undertones. Whitescar edged forward, checking the trail closely as he went. He lifted up his head again to see a large rift in the cliff face. It had been completely invisible from the base of the ridge, only revealing its presence to him when he was in exactly the right position.

'That's a relief. I didn't really fancy climbing over that!'

Whitescar scrambled over the last few boulders and edged cautiously into the mouth of the fissure. The cool breeze strengthened and so too did the smell of fresh water. Although there was only one way to proceed, he still checked the trail at regular intervals just to make certain. Now was not a good time to start taking things for granted.

Winding through the narrow rift in the hillside, Whitescar began to hear the sound of running water. Moments later, he was standing at the foot of the high waterfall with droplets of cool clean water falling onto his fur. For the first time in his life, Whitescar was glad to be getting wet. At the small pool next to the pathway, he stopped to drink, just as Raven had done. Every lap of the water was sheer bliss and at that moment, water had never tasted better. Whitescar began to relax again and even took time out for a quick wash.

'It's important to make a good first impression. I can't turn up looking like something I might have dragged in.'

By now, he was more than halfway through his journey but Whitescar knew that there was still a long way to go before he could rest. He also knew that he needed to arrive before dawn broke. The exchange had always been made this way. While the wizard slept, the changeover would take place, ensuring an unbroken line of familiars to assist the long line of Grimdyke wizards. Fanciful daydreams of magical spells and journeys on Barren Moor filled Whitescar's mind. He had spent the past seven long years preparing for his time at Greyfell Croft, trying to imagine what it would be like to work with the most powerful and respected wizard in the fells. How long his enthusiasm would last, only time would tell for Whitescar, the time ahead would test his loyalty.

The long winding rift appeared to go on forever. At every twist and turn, Whitescar expected to see the croft and the view across Barren Moor but he was not yet there. High above him, he thought he could see the sky but from the moment he entered the rift, he might as well have been in a tunnel or cave because the sky was cloudless and moon-shy and only a handful of stars could be seen from his position deep within the hillside. At long last, the ravine began to lighten and Whitescar hoped he was not too late. He quickened his step, now firmly convinced that there could be only one way in and one way out of the fissure. Suddenly, around the next sharp bend in the path, he got his first view over Barren Moor. Pools and bog water glistened in the distance as they reflected the stars in the sky above. The moor was bare, almost featureless and certainly lived down to its name. Again, Whitescar shook himself.

'It will look different in the daylight,' he told himself.

Over on the far hill, the light from the rising sun was just brushing the crest of the ridge. He had only minutes left, now he had to run and trust to instinct that he was still on the right track. Out of the hillside, he sped and down the short scree blanket to the foot of the ridge. Luckily, the trail was still fresh and following it came easy. In the distance, he could just make out the outline of a small croft against the darkness. For the first time, Whitescar could now see the long lines of drystone walls and small cart tracks that bounded the moor. In the distance, he could see the smoke rising from the croft fire and he knew that the start to his new life was just moments away. He continued to follow Raven's trail right to the garden wall, then jumping onto it, he got his first real look at the croft.

'Well, it's not as grand as I expected, maybe it's nicer inside.' Whitescar picked up the trail again only to realise that he would not be entering the croft through its front door.

'Surely not the servants' entrance?' he wondered, 'maybe some kind of secret entrance reserved for familiars.'

He padded excitedly round to the back of the cottage, across the small cobbled yard and up to the back door.

'Ah that's more like it, a *magic* door.'

Whitescar touched the panel of the cat-flap and it swung freely back and forth.

'Ingenious and typically wizard-like! Right Scar, this is it. The proud name of the colony is on your shoulders now so don't dog it up!'

He pushed open the flap and silently entered the croft. Whitescar's senses were immediately assailed by an overpowering mixture of smells and sensations. Peat smoke hung heavy in the air and the smell of discarded food then met his sensitive nose.

'I hope that's not *my* dinner!'

The air was alive with the presence of magic and once again, the fur on the back of his neck stood on end. He could see his new master's bed and in it, the outline of the wizard with whom he would spend the next seven electrifying years of his life. It was at that moment that Whitescar noticed that the tingle of magic he had felt was not actually coming from his new master as he first thought but from the croft itself as if the very stones of the building were charged with unseen power.

'This is going to be GREAT!'

Then he realised that he should be quiet and returned to the task of sniffing-out Raven's old sleeping quarters. They would be his now and he was expecting something quite special considering the role he was to play. The trail led him into the kitchen and to an old cardboard box located in the corner under a chair.

'This can't be right. Maybe it has some special properties that can only be appreciated from the inside.'

Whitescar leapt nimbly inside. The smell of singed fur was overpowering, it mingled with other odd smells but it was *definitely* where Raven slept. Whitescar tried to settle down, but found it more difficult than he had expected.

'Tomorrow is the big day. As tradition dictates, the Master will wake and greet me with the traditional greeting, after which he will cast his spell of protection over me and we can start doing MAGIC!'

Silas grunted again from underneath the covers and Whitescar clamped a paw over his mouth, not wishing to start his time badly by waking his master too soon. He turned around in the box and tried to settle.

'Small, but cosy, slightly smelly but oddly familiar … it will do, for now.'

After three more rotations in the box and a few more stamps and tramples with his paws, the bed was ready for use. Whitescar finally settled down and the exertions of the long night quickly carried him to sleep. All was quiet and peaceful, until …

'I'm sorry my friend … but I needed some way to warn you …'

83

'Raven? Is that you?'

Whitescar quietly drifted off again, while from the far end of the croft, Silas turned over and grumbled in his sleep.

'This humble box is the only sanctuary I could safely leave behind. It will protect you when times get rough … and I fear they might.'

'Raven? Where are you?' Whitescar mumbled again in his half-awake, half-asleep state.

'Good luck and safe nights, my friend.'

Whitescar heard no other voices during the night but the strange words he had heard, stayed with him until morning.

CHAPTER SEVEN
Ethan's Message

Dawn broke and for Whitescar, it felt as if all his birthdays had come at once. Like an overexcited kitten, he peered over the lip of the box, filled with anticipation.

'I wonder what his first spell of the day will be ... a bowl of food for me perhaps or a clean-up spell, the croft could certainly do with it. It could be something for the villagers, maybe a draught to cure a sick animal or he might enchant a hen so that it lays more eggs. I wonder what *my* first job will be.'

A stream of endless possibilities raced through Whitescar's head as he fixed his gaze on his new master's bed and watched for the first signs of movement. Patiently he waited as the sunlight began to pour in through the dirty windows of the croft. In the harsh light of day, the rooms looked even worse than they had done the night before. Whitescar wondered if he should make a start on cleaning the place but he was unsure of the best spell to use. Luna had taught him all the spells Ethan had passed to him. These were of course non-verbal spells or those that could be cast in felish. As Whitescar considered which pile of rubbish he should attempt to evaporate first, he began to suspect that there might be something wrong with his new master.

Now growing slightly concerned, he climbed out of his box and walked over to where the wizard was asleep on the large wooden bed in the main bedroom. The sheets were tatty and covered with cobwebs and Whitescar considered how long the wizard might have been lying there. Cobwebs draped the bedposts, the canopy above and hung from the pillows and down to the stone floor below.

'This is not what I expected at all!'

Whitescar then climbed on top of the bed and carefully picked his way through the nets of dusty webs until he could see the face of his master.

'He's not as old as I thought he would be but he's certainly a lot dirtier! Don't humans ever wash themselves? That mucky crust will take a lot of spit to clean off and just look at the tangles in his fur!'

Whitescar put a paw on Silas' beard and it crunched under his weight.

'Surely he can't be dead … can he? No, he's still breathing … *fhewee* and what breath! What *has* he been licking? This is all wrong. He's not at all how the others described him to me. Oh no! I'm not in the wrong croft, am I?'

Whitescar then ran out of the house through his 'magic' door and circled the croft.

'No, this is the place alright. Besides, Raven's box is in there. Maybe the master likes a wake-up call in the mornings … well, early afternoon. I think I should wake him, yes definitely. We're missing the best part of the day. Maybe then he'll do a wash-spell and get cleaned up.'

Whitescar ran back into the house and onto the bed where Silas had still not stirred. Then he considered how he should best tackle the next step. Whatever he chose to do, he had better get it right or his master would have his wand out before he could say, "watch where you're pointing that thing!" Whitescar made his move and put a paw on Silas' forehead … nothing happened. He backed off again and pummelled the sheets above Silas' chest, kneading them with his feet … still nothing. He then slapped his paw firmly on Silas' nose but apart from turning on his side, Silas was unresponsive.

'This calls for drastic action!' Whitescar thought and turned his attention to the bottom end of the bed.

Two dirty feet poked out from beneath the worn blankets and they gave Whitescar an idea. From the corner of the bed, he reached out a paw and carefully drew his longest claw down the entire length of Silas' bare foot.

'ARRGHH!' *Now* Silas was awake.

Whitescar bolted for the cover of his box and waited to see what would happen next. When he next looked out of his box he could see that the cobwebs had all gone and the bed was now *slightly* cleaner than before.

'Ah, a tidy spell!'

Actually, Silas had been dreaming about his hopeless situation, trapped inside the old, crumbling croft and the bleakness of his future, and the spells he mumbled had created centuries of cobwebs to complement his mood. At the precise second he awoke, the spells were all broken and the cobwebs and *some* of the dust vanished into smoke. Together with the half-remembered dream, they had disappeared leaving little trace. Whitescar studied the figure of Silas as he made his way into the kitchen to wash.

'This new master *acts* like an old man but surely he's too young. Either this is the result of some great and powerful restorative spell or ... oh no!' An alternative explanation then occurred to Whitescar. 'The warning last night, it wasn't Raven's voice I heard, it was Master Ethan's. The old wizard has ... gone! Why didn't Raven warn me? This is a disaster. I was preparing to join Ethan and now I've got the son, Silas. Why didn't Raven say something, he just let me run off into the darkness ... oh, I suppose that's why, I just ran away. I didn't give him the chance to warn me. Oh Scar, you dog-bone. What have you let yourself in for now?' Then he tried to rally his spirits. 'Come on snap out of it. The new master has probably been trained by Ethan in the same way Luna trained me. No need to panic, first things first, I had better introduce myself and get some food organised. I'm starving!'

Whitescar slipped out of his box and as Silas began to wash at the stone sink in the kitchen, he wound himself around his legs in the traditional cat greeting.

'Get away you flea-bitten reject! Get back into your ...' Feeling a stronger than expected push against his legs, Silas stopped and looked down to his feet and at Whitescar. 'Good grief! You've put some weight on over night!' Wiping the soap from his face and eyes, he got a better look at the cat, after which he quickly checked the calendar in the potion's cupboard.

'So that's why old Raven was getting so itchy, he couldn't wait to leave! This must mean that you're the new guy.'

Whitescar stood to attention, tail high in the air and chest out proudly.

'You look like you eat more than me! You must be twice the size of that old hearth-rug, Raven.'

Despite his keenness and his willingness to overlook the obvious, a few of Silas' comments were getting through to Scar and he did not like what he was hearing.

'My name is Whitescar and I am to be your new familiar,' he announced proudly. Silas took no notice. 'I am Raven's replacement ... so, where should I start?'

'I don't know what all that meowing and whining is about but if you're after food, you'll get what's left after I've eaten.'

Whitescar was stunned. Had he not made himself perfectly clear? He tried one last time but again his polite introduction was met with the same response.

'Cat, what *is* that on your chest, some sort of stain?'

'Stain? ... STAIN! What are you talking about? This is the mark of my family line!'

'Oh, don't start that caterwauling again, my head still hurts from all the bog-grog.'

'Do I even want to know what that is?' Whitescar sighed.

'It looks like a seagull got you from a great height!' Silas laughed. Then he looked a little closer at the crescent shaped mark on Whitescar's chest. Something about the moon symbol stopped Silas from continuing his rant and at the same time, he stopped laughing at the unfortunate cat. 'So, *Scar*, I expect you're another from that colony of miners' rejects come here for free food. Well anyone that stays here has to earn their keep and you'll be no exception!'

'He doesn't even understand felish. What else doesn't he understand?'

From that moment on, his proud name was reduced to simply, Scar, and more by luck than anything else, a name to which he had become accustomed from his time with Luna.

'Your first job after breakfast ...'

'Don't you mean dinner?' Scar muttered bitterly.

'I don't believe it! Don't tell me I'll have to put up with you muttering under your breath the way old Raven used to do? Just my luck!'

'Your luck? How about mine! I was supposed to start working with a great wizard today, and all I got was you ... whatever *you* turn out to be.'

'Shut up!' Silas snapped. 'Good, that's better. All right, first food, then out onto the moor where you can start gathering the ingredients needed to fill up the potions jars. They're all labelled so you can start as soon as you've eaten. Then we'll see if you earn your supper!'

'What about tea or is tea off for the staff?'

As Scar watched Silas eat, he licked his lips and drank a lot from the water bowl to stop his stomach gurgling. After a long wait, all that he had been left was the rind off Silas' bacon and some white from an egg.

'Welcome to the high-life Scar!' He was too hungry to argue and ate the scraps in a matter of seconds. 'Oh, I'm going to pay for eating that rubbish later. I thought I'd be eating better than this at Highfell ... what am I saying, I ate better than this at the forge!'

After licking the plate clean, apart from a dollop of dodgy looking brown sauce, Scar looked around the croft to locate the potions cupboard. First, he climbed the chair that stood in front of the large wall-hung cupboard. Then, after prising open the doors with a claw, he got his first look inside. Jars, bottles, packets and strange instruments filled the entire space, although most of the containers were empty. Scar looked at the fading calendar and immediately noticed the date and the fact that Raven had ringed it with a scratch. Scar looked down the long chart, counting off the years and looking for his own retirement date. When he at last found it, he too ringed it with a deep scratch from his claw.

'That is a long, long ... long way away,' he sighed, 'but whatever this new wizard is like, I can't let the colony down. I'll do my part as long as he does his. After all, he is still a Grimdyke.' Scar reluctantly returned to the task of restocking the potions cupboard. 'Right, what do we need ... oh, only *everything*. Better do this methodically so I'll start at the top and work down.'

Over the years, the Grimdyke wizards had become used to working with their familiars and had developed a system that suited both their needs. Each jar or box was carefully labelled and each label bore a full description of the contents. First, there was a drawing of the plant, grass or root, then below it, the name but it did not stop there. The pictures were specially designed for cats and were in fact, scratch and sniff! In addition, a small symbol at the bottom of the label explained what time of year the contents could be found in flower or at their most potent. Sadly, the well-intentioned plan had not been properly maintained and most of the labels had lost much of their sniff.

'First one ...' Scar scratched and then sniffed carefully. 'No way, not that one, he can't expect me to carry that! I'll try the next ... Oh this just gets better and better.'

Listed as "Purple" and "Yellow Aconite", the first plants on Scar's list were the deadly monkshood and wolfsbane, the third was the relatively harmless, bog asphodel. He made a mental note of the other plants needed to fill the first row of jars and then headed for his magic door and the moors beyond.

'Where am I supposed to find all these, some of them don't even grow on the moors!'

'And before you start moaning about how hard you have to work or where the plants and herbs are to be found, you have the whole of Barren Moor to choose from and the gardens and vegetable plots of the villagers so no excuses. Right, I think that's all you need to know, just remember, if you want to eat, you need to find the ingredients. Potions don't make themselves you know ... no ingredients, no food ... oh, I almost forgot.' Silas reached into his pocket and withdrew a small collar with a medallion hanging from it. He quickly fastened it around Scar's neck before he could complain. 'If you're lucky, this might just stop the villagers from shooting you when you're plundering their vegetable plots or herb gardens! You must wear it when you are near the village. Listen to me, talking to the great pudding of a cat like he can actually understand me!' Silas laughed. 'I'll take it off again each time you come home ... I don't want you losing it ... do you understand?' Then Silas laughed again.

'Oh, I can understand you alright, a lot better than you can understand me mate, which is probably just as well. I don't think you would like some of the things I've been calling you.'

Scar could not decide if Silas had heard or understood any of what he was saying or if it was the memory of Raven that had jogged something in Silas' mind but at least he had his answer. He also realised that his time with Silas was not going to be the great adventure for which he had hoped.

'Right, what did Luna say? Everything on the moor will want to eat me and the villagers will try to shoot me … it could be worse but I'm not sure how.'

Now totally disgruntled, Scar barged his way through the cat-flap and out into the garden beyond where he could calm down again in the fresh air before setting off in search of his first set of ingredients. He already knew about the protection charm cast over Greyfell Moor and it now appeared that there was a similar spell protecting the croft garden but beyond the drystone walls of the croft, danger lurked at every turn. Scar also suspected that he would need to hunt for most of his food on the moors if he wanted to avoid starving to death so if there was a silver lining to be found in his new situation, he had not yet discovered it.

'Well, a moor is a moor and I know what to expect, apart from predators that is but there are few to threaten a cat,' Scar recalled Luna's wise words, '… at least I hope that's true.' Scar thought about his list then he leapt onto the stone wall to survey the moor. 'Well this place lives down to its name alright, even in the daylight. Ok, back to the list and if I'm to carry all these poisonous plants back to Silas, I'm going to need something to carry them in.'

Scar searched the banks and pathways for a special plant. He was looking for some large dock leaves. He could use the broad leaves to wrap the more dangerous plants and then if he was careful, he could gently carry them back to the croft. After that, Silas could take care of them and fill the jars himself. All Scar would need to remember was to wash his paws well after handling them and not to eat any part of his deadly cargo as he harvested or carried it home.

'I've just realised. He's sent me out without using the protection charm on me. Either he *really* doesn't like me or he has no idea how it's done, either way that can't be good for me. What was it Ethan said about my sleeping box … maybe that's the only protection I'll have while I'm here. Oh wait … this is what I'm looking for.'

Scar carefully selected the largest of the dock leaves and after rolling them into a neat bundle with his paws, he picked them up and headed onto the moor. The first item from this list that he found was bog asphodel and luckily, it was not actually in the bog. Scar gently teased the pretty, orange-flowered plant out of its home in the damp peaty ground and wrapped it in the first of the broad dock-leaves.

'One down … loads to go and they get *really* nasty after this.'

Despite the threat of being shot, after Scar had collected a few more items from his list, he realised that he would need to try closer to the village. If he could avoid making contact with any of the armed farmers, he might just get away with all his nine lives intact. The bundle of plants was growing and there were still two more to find. First Scar carefully searched the abandoned allotments around the outskirts of Skelside village but with little success. There was only one option left to him, he would need to try the cottage gardens themselves.

Everything appeared to be going well until one of the local cats chanced upon him as he was searching. Immediately the cat identified Scar as an outsider and began to hiss and spit. Scar was not remotely concerned by the stranger's attitude; he had been trained to deal with far worse than a hissing fur-ball.

'What no introduction, no "Hi I'm Tiddles, who are you?" … typical, but at least he hasn't got a gun!'

The cat hissed and spat some more and although half Scar's size, it appeared he was not about to back down.

'Hush, Sebastian!' a strange human called to the hissing, spitting, ball of aristocratic fur. Then the young girl turned to Scar. Just to be on the safe side, Scar arched his back in an attempt to look even bigger. 'Silly cat, you don't need to be afraid of me.' Then the girl scratched the top of Scar's head.

'Well I don't know about villagers that carry guns but I like this!'

Scar rolled his head and enjoyed the scratch. At that moment, the bundle of flowers and roots fell from his mouth and onto the ground. The girl made to pick it up but Scar quickly pinned it to the ground with one of his large paws.

'Alright you can keep it. I wasn't going to steal it.' Then she recognised one of the flowers inside the dock-leaf bundle. 'You really shouldn't be carrying these in your mouth.'

'No? I'll put them in my shopping bag then ... no wait, I don't have one, because I'm only a CAT!' Scar snapped sarcastically.

'I'm sorry, I don't really speak felish that well. The wizard Ethan did try to teach me but it was very difficult.'

Scar sat down and stared at the girl in disbelief. Maybe he had been a little hasty. This human was actually being nice to him. Scar felt a bit ashamed also he felt that he could get to like the attention. It was at that moment, the girl noticed the small medallion hanging from the collar around his neck.

'I should have guessed. You're from Highfell Croft, aren't you? We're not supposed to go there anymore. Silas tried to banish us from the moor but it didn't work very well. We just stay away now because he a right miserable old dog!'

Scar laughed. It appeared he was not the only one to hold Silas in low regard.

'So you understand some of what I'm saying at least. Wait here. I have an idea. I won't be a minute. Just talk to Sebastian while I'm gone.'

The girl disappeared in the direction of the cottage, leaving Scar with the slightly superior looking Persian cat.

'Parlez-vous felish?' Scar asked, in a clumsy "English cat abroad" sort of way.

'No, of course not!' Sebastian replied firmly.

'Sorry I just thought ... wait a minute, how do you know what I said then?'

'I'm only pulling your lead. Of course I speak felish, we all do in the village. A few of us even understand human, Ethan taught us before he left. Sometimes I have quite long conversations with my owner, April.'

'You're *owned* by her! ... What, like slavery?'

'No, you're thinking of dogs. I stay with her because we get along well together. You're a feral, aren't you, no wonder you don't understand.'

'I'm Silas' new familiar and it's the first time I've stayed with a human,' Scar replied.

'You get used to them eventually, their funny noises and the way they smell. April looks after me if I'm ill and she feeds me when I get hungry. It took me a while to train her but she's coming along fine now. I don't envy you though, if you're staying with Silas. He's not exactly cat friendly ... he's not exactly *anything* friendly!' Sebastian laughed.

'I'm Whitescar but my friends call me Scar, oh and so does Silas but *how* he guessed I've no idea.'

Just then, April returned with something in her hand.

'It's not much but I think it will be safer than holding the plants in your mouth, even though you have shown the good sense to wrap them first. I need to adjust it before it will fit properly so while you wait you can join Seb in a snack while I adjust the strap.

Both cats immediately began to wind around April's legs, having spotted the food bowl in her other hand.

'I told you some of them were Ok!' Sebastian said purring.

April gave them both a good scratch on their heads as they ate and then she set about making the necessary adjustments. When she had finished she presented Scar with a small tube shaped, plastic container. It had a strap that would fit easily and comfortably around his neck so that the bag hung by his shoulder.

'All you need to do is put the plants into the tube and then push your head through the strap to carry them home, *simples*!' April squeaked. 'Sorry, that's another creature altogether!' then she giggled.

'No even I didn't understand that one,' Sebastian replied to Scar's puzzled looks.

Scar studied his new plant collector's bag. After a few sniffs to check it out, he tried it on for size. It was perfect and it would easily carry all the specimens he had gathered. April went to pick up the leaf wrapped plants but again Scar put his oversized paw on the bundle to stop her.

'It's alright, I know that they're dangerous but I'm a little surprised to see that you do. You must be a very clever cat.' April smiled and rubbed Scar's chin. 'If you let me put them in the bag for you, I'll go and wash my hands after … Ok?'

Scar lifted up his paw and April placed the samples in the bag for him. Scar half wished he was staying with April now, instead of Silas but he had his job to do and after all, it was only for seven years.

'Seven years! It's going to feel like a forever-pain!' he sighed.

'You can always come and visit us. You will always be welcome here. Seb tells me your name is Scar. Is that because of the moon shaped white patch on your chest? I'll bet your full name is something like …' April thought for a moment and Sebastian rubbed against her leg as she sat and studied her new cat acquaintance. '…Whitescar?'

'Did you tell her Seb?' Scar asked accusingly.

'No he didn't,' April interrupted, 'I told you I could speak a little felish … well, *understand* some of it. I can't actually speak it *properly*. It's just that you have such a strong accent and it was a little difficult at first. It probably came from all those years spent with the miners.'

'I have to go now,' Scar explained. 'If I don't return with the plants, Silas will go dog-doo on me!'

April laughed.

'Sorry that was rude. I don't normally use language like that; it's just that he's so, so …'

'I know Scar. Just keep your head down and stay on your guard. I'd like to see you again sometime.'

Scar pushed his head through the loop on his new collector's bag and picked up his delivery for Silas. He then rubbed around April's legs one more time before heading off for the moors and back to Highfell Croft.

As Scar glanced back towards the garden he could see Sebastian watching and April waving, then he turned bounded onto the moor heading for his new home with Silas.

Time for Scar dragged by slowly and Silas' attitude towards him got worse if anything. As well as casting the occasional spell in his direction, Silas was prone to kicking him out of the way when he found himself in the wrong place at the wrong time. Scar was thoroughly miserable. To cheer himself up a little, he made a point of calling on April when he was foraging on the moor for plants to fill the potions jars. He liked the way she talked *to* him and not *down* to him … the food she often gave him was nice too.

Night time was the worst time for Scar but at least he knew he was safe in his protected box. Night after night, he would watch in despair and trepidation as all manner of conjured up creature was set free to roam the cottage. Furniture would disappear in the blink of an eye and spectres, goblins and ghouls would wail in the night keeping him awake. In the morning, when Silas awoke, all would return to normal, except for Scar's memories and his shattered nerves. He had thought of sleeping in the garden but his box would not fit through the magic door. It was becoming clear to him that his master was a pale imitation of the old wizard but he had no idea how to help. Silas was also very rude to him, sometimes even cruel and if it were not for April, he probably would have starved by now.

Minutes felt like hours, and hours more like weeks, and all Scar could do now was grit his teeth and try to accept his fate.

CHAPTER EIGHT
Becky and Nightfire

While Scar hunkered down, trying to be the best familiar he could despite Silas, Nightfire and Becky were continuing their own journey of discovery. As Becky's play turned to more grown-up thoughts, Nightfire was frequently joined by Luna and even Raven when he was not with his charge, the oddly named, Nappa. She was so called because of her strange ability to fall asleep anywhere. Nappa, the young female, had been chosen as Whitescar's replacement and her training with Raven had just begun in earnest. Now with two uncles and one older brother both watching over her and training her, Becky was seen in a new light. Nightfire and Luna both felt an unexpected responsibility for her and as a result, all the little bits of magic they had retained, they passed on to Becky. For whatever reason, Nightfire remembered nearly all of his time with Ethan; including the many spells and potions he had been taught. Luna found that he too was having frequent flashbacks to the old days, and at such times, he could clearly recall his master's training as if it were only yesterday.

Raven was still working with his new charge, Nappa, the kit that would grow to be Whitescar's replacement. As a result, he was able share his understanding of magic with both students, something that had never before been done. Nappa of course took priority but while the spells and potions still lingered in Raven's memory, he passed on what he could to Becky.

Unless Raven's duties took him elsewhere, the three ex-familiars would take it in turn to walk with the young Becky and when they could, they would tell her about the great wizarding family and show her spells and concoctions that could turn foul water sweet, rid a bite of all its poison and show the truth in any deception. Becky learned fast, despite being small and female. The role of familiar traditionally went to a male but this was not without exception. The very first cat from their colony to join Ezra Grimdyke was a female. She was called Bess and she was as black as the darkest night and as sharp as a new claw. Little had been beyond her grasp and her keen instincts had protected Ezra during her seven-year stay with him. Nightfire never underestimated the intelligence of the female of his kind, particularly the strength and determination shown by a queen. He had seen a female protect her young against a fox attack and prove victorious ... no, they were not called queens by accident. They were resourceful, smart and resolute. Yet with all his understanding and respect for the female of his species, Nightfire still could not put his paw on what was so different about his young niece, Becky.

Much to their surprise, for every new thing they would teach her, be it spell or incantation, Becky could still show them two things that were new. She had three experienced familiars to teach her but she had something more on her side. Over the past seven years, Becky had earned the trust of most creatures that lived on Greyfell Moor. She knew their native tongue and could converse quite freely with most of them, often to their great surprise. What she got in return was their unique view of life on the moors. The moles that lived on the drier fringes of the fell told her of life beneath the grassland and the mysterious underground places they had visited. The songbirds painted pictures of the world as they saw it. Their view from high above gave Becky a far more detailed impression of the world in which she lived. From these shared experiences, Becky had been able to build up a mental map of the area, one worthy of the oldest and greatest explorers of her colony. She learned to understand the watercourses from the water voles and the runs and pathways of the moor from her many other four-legged friends. Becky had developed a *oneness* with all about her, an ability that Nightfire could only marvel at and quietly envy. Sometimes, as he talked with her, it felt as if he were talking to his old master, Ethan. Becky certainly appeared to have wisdom beyond her years.

It was from her talks with the other creatures of the fells and moors that Becky had developed a deep understanding of plants and grasses. Her potion-brewing skills were soon beyond anything Nightfire, Luna or Raven had been taught. In fact, she was frequently called on to administer to wounded animals, creatures that would normally shy away from cats for fear of being devoured by them. Becky had won their trust in a way only matched by the great wizard Ezra himself. Yet with all her natural ability, one thing still eluded Becky, she could not cast spells. All except the most basic felish charms were beyond her but what she lacked in spell casting she more than made up for with her liquid magic. Tinctures, concoctions, elixirs, brews and tisanes, Becky knew them all and with her special brand of potions, she was second to none, except the great Wizard himself of course.

One day, as Nightfire and Luna watched from afar, a small bank vole was brought nervously to Becky, by two attendants. Nightfire's thoughts about the strange affair were plain; Luna clearly heard his stomach rumble.

'I'll never understand why she plays with her food like that,' Luna admitted.

'*I'll* never understand how she can lick a creature's fur clean without eating it!' Nightfire replied. 'But she tends to them as if they were her own. I've observed her cleaning wounds, drawing poison from bites and stings, even helping with their newborn … it's incredible really. And yet she still cannot cast a proper spell, except in felish!'

The pair looked on in awe and disbelief as the vole was treated with plant and root extracts and sent on its way again.

'What a waste of talent …' Luna exclaimed.

'What a waste of food!' Nightfire added as he watched the potential snack run away and back to its home in the riverbank.

'But as the smallest of seven and a female, who would take Becky seriously?' Luna observed.

'Any that tried to separate her from one of her friends!' Nightfire replied grinning broadly. 'I saw her chase off one of the colony's large toms the other week, Six-claws I think it was. He was hungry and the mouse she was treating not yet fully recovered from its brief encounter with a kestrel. When Six tried to take the mouse from her, she went berserk! She flew at him spitting and cursing all kinds of ills and at one point, I swear I saw the fur on Six's tail catch light! She may not be the biggest cat in the colony but she is determined and resourceful beyond her size and rarely have I seen her back down, only when there was no other course of action open to her. Even when she is on the attack, her wit and not her temper guide her.'

'Does she still swim in the stream?' Luna asked casually.

'Every day. She is the only cat I have ever seen that is equally at home in or out of the water. Leah gave birth to an oddity in that one but I would not have her any other way. It's just that …'

'… The others don't see her the same way?' Luna suggested.

'I think they are a little scared of her. At first, they used to laugh but few laugh at her now. She has won most of them round and although they don't fully understand what she does, at least they show her some respect, the ones who still talk to her that is.'

'The others still think that she's as mad as a bag of wet mice!' Luna laughed.

'At least they don't pick on her any more.'

So, this was to be Becky's lot. Half the colony thought she was a strangely reclusive cat, the rest thought she was either mad or a witch. Becky did not mind either way. She was happy with who she was ... more or less.

As time passed, Nightfire and Luna taught her all that they knew, as for the rest, that would only come with experience. Becky however, had not yet finished with their education and she still had much to teach them in return for their belief in her. The old toms of the colony still regarded most of her patients as easy snacks but for her sake, they refrained from eating them. Nightfire's biggest problem now was what happened next. The more Becky retreated alone on the moors the fewer friends she kept amongst the colony. Nightfire feared that she was destined to become some kind of ridiculed hermit.

Meanwhile, Raven's training of the eager young kit, Nappa, was beginning to show results. She did however have one slightly annoying habit. She had the tendency to disappear on starlit nights, causing Raven great concern when trying to find her in time for her lessons. It appeared that she had a thing about stars and would frequently go to sleep on her back while studying them. During such times, she was able to conjure a powerful, natural inconsequence that made her almost invisible to anyone trying to find her. It was clear to Raven that this natural gift would stand her in good stead as a familiar, *when* she learned to control it.

'She'll be a great familiar,' Raven explained proudly, 'and her ability to disappear might just save her from Silas.'

Yes, there was still the matter of Silas to be addressed. One night, as Raven toiled with his new apprentice and Luna patrolled the moors, Nightfire sat with Becky and they talked about the future.

'I don't really think about it. I only think about the now,' Becky replied.

'But I've watched you; you do far more than that.'

'I see shapes from the past in the mist that hangs over the moors and images of the future that form from stars reflected in the pools but it is now that matters the most.'

'Are you happy with now?'

'I'm needed and that makes me happy.' Becky then thought for a moment before continuing. 'I hope you don't mind but on the days when you or Luna aren't with me, I've been teaching one of the other cats some of the things I have learned.'

'That is strictly the job of a retired familiar. It not a suitable job for …'

'But you don't see the things I see or hear the words I hear from the other creatures. You can't teach what I know!'

Slowly the anger in Nightfire's chest subsided and as the light in his eyes dimmed, he looked again at the cat sitting bravely in front of him. If any other had made the same suggestion he would have slapped them across the muzzle but in his heart he knew that she was right and despite tradition, she and only she could pass on the things she had learned. Nightfire took in a deep breath and settled down again. He could smell sweet water running in the stream, the grass and the heady perfume of the night flowers. He could even hear two hedgehogs as they watched from the cover of some tall grass. What was even more surprising was that he could even catch the odd word of their conversation.

'He's familiar, old … retired,' one hedgehog commented to the other.

'She talks to animals … helped some she has.'

'I heard … saved … old weasel!'

'No! … Odd things, cats.'

The odd chattering noises actually made sense, now that his mind was clear and open to new ideas.

'Alright, which of the colony has been brave enough to visit you on the moors?'

'She's called Tabitha,' Becky replied then she braced herself for his reaction.

'But that's a ...' Nightfire took a deep breath and began again. 'She can't be from our colony, that's a human given. Don't tell me she's an indoors cat!'

'No, her family used to live with the miners, just like we did, only when the miners left the valley, her forefathers stayed on. Even when our colony left the miners' village, they stayed. They found food and shelter in the old inn. It's not her fault that the colony she lives with decided to keep human given names. She's still feral at heart, like any of us.'

Nightfire had heard that some of the original cats had chosen to stay on but no one knew what had become of them. The two colony's paths never crossed again after they had separated. Nightfire thought for a moment.

'At least Tabitha is not a *fancy* breed from the village. They're too moody for words. How is she doing, this new pupil of yours?' he asked.

'Tabitha is a quick learner and she's even picking up some of the other tongues now but there is something else.' Whatever it was, Nightfire sensed that it was not good. 'One of the reasons she wanted to learn other ways of talking was because she met a wild cat called Silver that lives on the high moors and peaks.'

'She's mixing with a dangerous breed there. All *they* know is hunting and killing. You should warn your new friend to stay away, they're a bad lot.'

'Tabitha says this one is alright, he's not as wild as the others, actually, I don't think he's a real wild cat at all, just one

105

from the old settlement that has chosen to live alone. Tabitha says he's all right with her, it's humans he really doesn't like.'

'So what has this to do with languages?'

'Tabitha has been able to learn to speak wild-felish, well whatever it is that Silver speaks, it's not all that different really and she's been teaching me in exchange for me teaching her other animal talk. The point is that Silver has been forced to visit the village, because food has been scarce for him and while he was there, he saw other cats.

'Becky, this tale sounds like it could go on for a whole season, is there a point to any of this?'

'While he was there he came across another cat called Sebastian ...'

'I'll bet *he's* a breed with a name like that.'

'That's not the point. Sebastian is one of the village house cats ...'

'... Soft bunch!' Nightfire interrupted, Becky continued undeterred.

'Sebastian knows Whitescar. Silver told Tabitha that he heard Sebastian and Whitescar talking one day. Silver heard that Silas is putting my brother in danger.'

'What *exactly* did this wandering cat hear?'

'Whitescar has been collecting plants and roots from Barren Moor, some of them deadly dangerous.'

'So it has been for all of us. There's no news in that.'

'Whitescar has no spell of protection!'

'Impossible! The wizard always casts a protection charm over his familiar, how else could a cat expect to survive the spells and potions set against them by other dark wizards or the deadly effects of the potion ingredients he must collect. Either the breed or the wild one must have heard wrong, it is impossible.'

'Tabitha believes it to be true and Silver said that Whitescar was looking tired and thin.' Becky was clearly convinced that her brother was in danger.

Their thoughts turned to Whitescar and they wondered how he must be feeling, lumbered with a bad tempered and almost non-magical wizard. A familiar without a protection spell was at great risk but Nightfire could not allow his concern to show.

'He'll be fine, Luna has taught him well. You'll see in seven years, Whitescar will be back with tales of adventure and great magic.'

At that moment, they heard a strange noise. Something was skulking in the long grass. Fevered breathing and snorting could be heard coming from the other side of a small thicket of reeds. As Nightfire readied himself for the confrontation, his eyes glowed red in the darkness. Becky threw a small paw-full of green dust into the pool of water causing it to bubble and foam violently.

'That will force the creature into the open. The smell is unbearable to any moor dweller,' Becky explained.

Eventually a large black form crashed through the reeds, tumbling, falling towards Nightfire and Becky. Nightfire raised a paw to strike.

'Stop, it's ... Whitescar!'

'Impossible!' Nightfire replied. 'He still has six more years to complete.'

Nightfire turned over the lifeless body and suddenly the moonlight caught the white crescent patch on his chest.

'Scar!' Becky cried. Then she smelled his breath and felt his chest. 'Stay with him, there's something I must do.' Becky ran into the night leaving Nightfire with the lifeless body of Whitescar and an impossible puzzle to answer.

CHAPTER NINE
The First

As Nightfire waited, Scar's breathing grew shallower. Suddenly Becky returned with her mouth full of pungent plants and herbs.

'I hope I've got them all.' After spitting them onto the ground, she then began pounding the leaves with her paws. Soon the pulped green mixture was ready.

'Hold his head while I spread this onto his chest and then give him one of these seeds to eat ... only one, more and it will kill him for sure.'

Nightfire did as he was told and then sat back with Becky to see if they were in time. Scar's head rolled from side to side as the pungent fumes coming from the green poultice on his chest were slowly drawn into his lungs. He coughed and then gasped as if surfacing from a long swim under water. Scar's eyes flickered opened and then he was violently sick.

'What did you give him?' Nightfire asked Becky.

'I knew you hadn't taken it all in. I *did* tell you about the potion but it's a lot to understand in one lesson. You really need to practise more,' she replied thoughtfully. 'I think with time, you could do the same, if you are willing to try.'

Scar coughed again, straining his empty stomach.

'You should drink, Scar. Try this.'

Becky squeezed some damp sphagnum moss onto Scar's lips and he lapped at the clean, sweet water. Then, with Becky on one side and Nightfire on his other, they guided Scar to a nearby pool of clear water where he drank his fill.

'He's waterless ... his fur hangs loose on his bones,' Becky explained. 'This drink will probably come back too but the next should stay with him.'

She was right. Scar's first reaction was to hurl again but after, he appeared to brighten and his eyes began to grow clearer. Scar drank again and as he did, Becky brought a fish from the nearby stream for him to eat.

Some time later, as Scar's strength began to return, Becky gave him a different potion to take.

'Don't worry, this one won't make you sick, the worst is over. Now we need to build you up again.'

Scar ate the fish and the strange salad Becky had prepared for him.

'What is this, it tastes ... *odd*,' Scar croaked, his voice still a little hoarse.

'Just something to counter the last of the poison and the bad spells you have been fighting. Just eat now and worry about what it is later. We'll help you back to the colony then you can tell us what happened.'

'No! I can't go back. Just take me somewhere safe for now. I can never show my face in the colony again. When you know what I've done, you will understand why.'

'I know a place ... just beyond the forge, you'll be safe there but in the morning you must tell us why you have returned,' Becky said sternly.

Nightfire smiled at this new resolute side to his niece and as he watched her with Scar, some of the fears he held for her future were laid to rest. She was no longer the young and insecure recluse she once had been but a competent and resourceful cat, one Nightfire was proud to know. For the present, all they could do was wait with Scar. The morning would bring with it many new questions.

When dawn broke, Nightfire awoke to find a small collection of fish and some more of the strange salad Becky had given Scar the night before.

'You were both sleeping so soundly I didn't want to wake you,' Becky replied as she returned with yet another small fish. 'There's enough for all of us, even you need to eat, uncle.'

Scar stirred, disturbed by the sound of talking and the smell of fish.

'What happened?'

'You happened, on us last night, remember?' Nightfire replied.

'He probably won't remember much of last night. I gave him something to help him sleep,' Becky replied.

'Hello sis. I remember being given something that made me sick last night.'

'Whatever she gave you, it probably saved your life,' Nightfire replied with some pride.

'What, sis did that? I thought you were the familiar not her,' Scar replied slightly dismissively.

'She's no longer the cat you remember Scar, she has grown and learned well but now we need to know what happened to you and why in all these many long years, you are the first to return from Greyfell before time,' Nightfire said more softly.

As the three cats ate, Scar slowly began to open up to them and he told them of his ordeal at the hands of Silas and of the events that led to him returning in shame.

'I wasn't there long before I realised that there was something very wrong with Silas. Finding him in charge and not Ethan was a shock but finding that he was practically magic-less was an even greater shock. To begin with, I just followed orders and did my job but Silas was so bitter at not being powerful or respected, things just got worse. My very first job was to restock the potions cupboard and if it had not been for April and Sebastian ...'

'Sebastian, friend of Tabitha?' Nightfire asked.

'Yes. How on Grimdyke's beard do you know them?'

'It doesn't matter for now, carry on.'

'April gave me a bag to put the flowers in and Seb, that's Sebastian, he cleared it with the other cats so I could gather plants from their gardens without being attacked. To begin with it wasn't too bad but gathering the plants was slowly making me sick. Silas didn't know about the familiar's protection charm, did I tell you, he sent me out with no shield at all. I lived on my wits. I faced death from the sky, Big-eyes and hawks, angry sticks, sorry, snakes ... everything out there wanted to eat my food ... or me. I still remembered the things Luna taught me and I could even cast a few felish spells but that's when it really started to go wrong. I tried to evaporate a hissing stick ...'

'Snake!' Becky corrected. 'What kind?'

'What do you mean "what kind"! They're all the same aren't they? Hissy and stick-like! Anyway, I ran into one, one day ... *literally*, ran straight into it. Boy that was one hissed-off stick. Before I could run away, it bit my leg.'

'Can you describe it, the *stick* that bit you?' Becky said as she searched Scar for the wound. 'Was it about your length with a dark zigzag on its head and body?'

'It had some sort of dark line on its back ... I didn't stop to find out, why, does it matter?'

'Vipera!' Nightfire replied softly, 'but you already knew that, didn't you Becky?'

'I suspected as much when I saw the state he was in. That's why I gave him the potion to draw out the poison. This one will clean and protect his insides against further harm.' Becky then turned to Scar. 'The thing I don't understand is how you have survived this long.'

111

'When I was bitten, I was near to Seb's place and when I limped into his garden he got April and then April got a strange smelling human who gave me a prickled leg and something to drink. Both were *really* unpleasant! After that, I stayed a few days with Seb and April before I headed back to the croft. When I got back, Silas was *rabid*. I think he had been at the bog-grog. At first, he was shouting and smashing things but when he saw me, he started to wave his wand at me. He shouted all kinds of nonsense spells at me and with each failed spell, he grew even angrier. Eventually he remembered one from a dream and he shouted "eradico" and from his wand leapt an angry purple light and the chair next to me exploded and was gone!'

'He tried to kill you?' Becky asked in utter disbelief.

'Not deliberately, at least not at first. This was the first real spell I had ever seen him cast but it was not to be the last. Following this success, he then exploded nearly everything in the croft and soon I had nowhere left to hide. Then the peat basket I was hiding in suddenly exploded and I was left in an empty room with nowhere to go.'

'What happened next?' Nightfire enquired.

'Silas screamed, "Now I have you, flea-bag" and he raised his wand again.'

'What did you do?' Becky asked.

'I suddenly remembered something you taught me, a spell in felish. "Contego", I shouted, and held out my paw. The purple light streaming angrily from Silas' wand hit my paw but it bounced off again, shattering his jars of bog-grog. The smelly, frothy liquor ran onto the floor dousing the fire. Silas looked back at me and raised his wand again but I dashed for my sleeping box and hid inside.'

'You hid in a box? But that meant you were trapped!' Nightfire exclaimed.

'Not trapped, not in there. The box was the only place I ever felt safe. When Silas saw I could do magic, no matter that it was only a simple defensive spell, he lost it completely. From inside my box I heard all kind of spells and curses being tried. My sleep-box jumped and rocked with every angry outburst. Through his anger, Silas tapped into his darker side and the spells he began casting were bad, *very* bad. This rage driven attack went on for most of the day and into the night. His spell casting ability grew as his anger took over him. I lost all track of the time but eventually, the croft grew quiet again. I think Silas had worn himself out.'

'What happened next?' Becky asked, by now she was close to tears, hearing what her brother had been forced to endure.

'I waited until I was sure, then I looked over the lip of the box. The room was full of smoke but little else; Silas had destroyed nearly everything in the croft. Looking around the room, I decided that Silas must have gone out. He used to go out into the night and evaporate bats and owls as they flew by. I used to hear him laughing outside and see the flashes from his wand through the windows. I just couldn't take any more and I knew if the protection spell on my sleeping-box ever failed or he caught me out in the room somewhere, he would kill me. I had to leave but I had nowhere to go. I didn't want to come back here to be the first to fail but if I went to the village, I knew he would track me down and I didn't want to lead him to my friends, Seb and April.'

'So you came here.'

'I tried. I had nothing to bring back with me, no possessions except for the collection bag April made for me, so I put some meat from the kitchen in it and set off for the magic door. Before I reached it, the door swung open and there was Silas, swaying, angry and full of bog-grog. He had stashed some of it away in the garden, a secret supply I didn't know about … I think he suspected that I was doing … *something* in it. Well I wasn't, not at first but then he made me so angry, well …' Scar chuckled, 'it's really bog-grog now!'

'Scar, you shouldn't have, not to a Grimdyke wizard,' Nightfire scolded whilst trying hard to hide a grin.

'He deserved it … he deserved more but I had nothing left, I couldn't fight him. My stomach hurt, my leg was sore and … anyway, I had to leave and let the colony down. It had all gone wrong. Between where I sat, cowering like a kit and freedom, stood Silas and he was not about to let me pass. He pulled his wand from inside his jacket and said quietly "I'm really going to enjoy this. It's about time you found out what you were up against!" and then he pointed his wand at me and yelled "ERADICO!" with a hatred and bitterness I have never seen before, not even in him. At the same time, I held my paw out and reached for my sleeping-box with the other to steady me as I called "CONTEGO" and then I braced myself for the end to come. Next, there was a blinding flash of purple light and a smell of burning and dried earth, along with a loud bang that made my ears whistle. Then ... nothing! I thought I was dead but when I could eventually open my eyes again Silas was lying on the floor and there was a large pile of smouldering dust where my sleeping-box had been. All of Ethan's magic that he had put into the box had joined with my small spell to protect me, and now it was all gone, the box, its protection charm and half the stones on the living room floor. All that was left was a small pile of dust that used to be my bed.'

Scar stopped talking and distractedly washed his paw. His mind was back in Highfell Croft reliving the moment he was sure he would die. Becky pushed some of the green herbs towards him and he ate them absentmindedly.

'You were telling us about when you left,' Nightfire prompted.

'Eh? Sorry, I don't know where I was then. Oh, the bang … the loudest bang. I looked over at Silas. Despite all he had done, I didn't want to be responsible for his death. I walked over to where he was lying and I could feel his breath on my whiskers. I couldn't hear him, my ears were still ringing from the blast. I could only think of one spell but it was not to heal just to repair but it was all I could remember. I put a paw on his head and said "renovo" I don't know if it did any good but it was all I could think of at the time.'

'It will do a little more than repair broken objects. You probably saved his life, Scar, and from what you have told us, none of this was your fault. He brought this on himself,' Nightfire said with great sadness in his voice. 'This is not what the old master wanted for the boy. Things have gone badly wrong at Highfell.'

'If only I had been there. With the right potion I could have healed him,' Becky added.

'It will take more than a backfired spell to destroy a Grimdyke, even one like Silas. I am sure that Scar did the right thing. Tell us, what happened next, Scar?' Nightfire needed to coax the whole story from Scar. Painful though it was, they all needed to be clear about the full picture.

'With Silas still in deepest sleep, I returned to the kitchen and gathered some more food. After that I took a few ingredients from the potions cupboard to make a wrap for my wounds. Then I headed out onto Barren Moor. By this time, it was growing dark and the first of the Big-eyes were already out hunting.'

CHAPTER TEN
Whitescar's Shame

'Between where I stood and the colony I longed to be with, lay the hunters of Barren Moor, the many deep dark pools of snag-weed and then Greyfell Moor beyond Highfell Ridge, it was going to be a long night, far longer than I thought.'

'When did you leave Greyfell?' Becky asked her brother as her concern began to grow.

'Three nights ago. I travelled for two nights and two days without rest ... well almost. I even flew part of the way!'

'WHAT?' Nightfire and Becky said in astonishment.

'That came later, on the second day. First, I had to cross Barren Moor to reach Highfell Ridge and that's when it began to get rough. The half-light of evening brings with it many creatures onto the moors. It's a time of great feeding ... and of being fed upon. The hissing sticks retreat as it grows cooler but the mice, voles and other small creatures that come out attract the larger predators. The sky fills with unseen dangers and the moors seethe with hunters, keen to fill their bellies. I tried to practise all that you had taught me but it was not enough. Even when I stalked as quietly as I knew how, there was always something following me. I was still weak from the stick-bite and after the blast from Silas' wand, a little head-spun too. I wandered Barren Moor for longer than I should have and angered many who live there. It's nothing like we are used to on Greyfell. Barren Moor is alive at night but not just with food as it is here. I think we have grown a little soft, Nightfire, I know *I* had.

As I travelled, creatures that would have ignored my company here began to see me as a threat or worse, as food. The weasels taunted me, some even tried to mesmerise me with their dance. I have seen them bewitch an animal ten times their size and render it docile, docile enough for them to kill and carry off to feed their young.'

Becky winced. She knew this kind of thing happened, her many animal friends had told her of life on other moors but it was a hard way of life and one she did not envy.

'Did you meet any other cats on the moor?' Becky then enquired in an attempt to change the subject.

'Not on the moor and none from our colony but descendants of some that followed the miners long ago, when they moved to Skellside. Descendants of those cats now have their home in the houses there, just as their ancestors had done in the miners' crofts of Greyfell Moor. They now hunt on Barren Moor but only for small fry and they always stay close to the village. I spent too long on that moor, yet found little to eat or drink that I did not have to fight hard for and any food I caught hardly made up for the effort of the kill. Worse still, my store of food in the collection bag contained little water and so I quickly grew thirsty. I had to stop and eat the food in my bag and rest. Having eaten a little, my head cleared again and as my senses returned, I realised my mistake. I had strayed away from the hill and towards the village. I now had further to go than when I set out.

'I turned again to face Highfell Ridge and the spot where I hoped to find the pass and then I began my trek across the full width of Barren Moor.' Scar shuddered at the memory.

Becky added a few seeds to the remaining fish and pushed it towards Scar. He ate but his thoughts still held his mind captive on the terrible moor. Gradually his mind cleared again as the potion Becky had added to the food took effect.

'Was it *really* bad on the moor?' Becky asked.

'I'd rather look back on my time there than look forward to doing it again. Yes, it was bad, and the moor now stood between where I was and the pass through Highfell Ridge. At first, the going was easy. The many tracks laid down by the village cats and even some of the children, made it clear which way was safe but their adventuring only helped me so far and soon the trails ended. I followed my nose and a line of sight to the pass but the moor was uneven and my view of the pass frequently disappeared. I ate what I could but sweet water was rare. Most of the pools there bring certain confoggation and death so I tried some of the wetter creatures for food.'

'You don't mean you ate the frogs!' Becky said sounding horrified by the thought.

'Frogs, newts, fish whatever I could find that was wet. Some of the frogs ... they made spells of their own. After eating one ... well, part of one, I saw the strangest things. First, I thought I was home and then I saw a huge food bowl filled with food just for me, but before I could feed, I was visited by the flying-death. To this moment, I am still not sure if they were real or part of my head-spin. I could no longer tell life from dream. Then the skies filled with talons, claws and terrible curved beaks, and I hid. I lay in a hollow on the moor and shook for hours. I don't know if it was fear or the bad pond creature I ate but I was sick. When my head-spin cleared again, I returned to the trail, what little I could find of it. You know, looking back I definitely think that frog was off.' Scar managed a weak laugh.

'Further along, I noticed a new threat. The foul-smelling bogs have fire-creatures lurking in them and bright lanterns dance across their surface. Once I thought it was a child from the village and I followed behind the light. Soon I was caught in the tangle-weed and fighting for my life. I had been tricked by the lantern and had wandered deep into a bog. The way out was difficult and all the time the gases made my head dull.

'The bogs and the lanterns were not the worst the moor sent to try me. Worst of all were the magical creatures. Attracted to the wizard's croft they came from far and wide. They gather at night to taunt white wizards, hoping to turn them but mainly just to have fun. If they can turn a wizard or kill them, they can steal their power. The first part of their plan seems harmless enough. They simply enchant objects so that they don't work or hide things you need. Some can even cast spells but none of them were friendly. I only caught glimpses of them on the moor but they were nothing like us. They were two-feet, like the master but very small and thin. Others were more like stick-hissers but they ran on legs, some even had *two* heads ... but I suppose it all could have been the pond creature I ate. All through the night, I wandered across the moor with little idea where I was heading but as dawn broke, my luck changed and I could see the pass through Highfell Ridge and it gave me new hope. I don't know what hand or scent had guided me but I could finally see a way off the terrible moors.

'By the time I had reached the foot of the rift, high up on the side of Highfell Ridge, I was hungry and thirsty but not as hungry as my stalker. I had felt its eyes on my back for most of the night; in fact, they had rarely left me. At first, I thought it was just the sickness or a trick of the moor but then I heard a cry, a loud scream high above me. I ran for the deep cut in the hillside, scrabbling over loose rocks and dead tree roots until I found cover. There I waited until it flew away again. After making sure the sky was clear, I set off again. I knew that there was fresh water further inside the pass but I was a long way from drinking it and I was so dry.'

Scar licked his lips unconsciously as he spoke.

'Water always runs in the rift, even in the driest of years,' Nightfire added knowledgeably. 'From where you stood, it could only have been an hour or so away.'

119

'When I was sure the flying-death had gone, I began walking again and wound my way through the cut in the hillside. I was so tired by that time and I was finding the way far harder than I remembered it, also, it was a lot further to sweet-water than I had hoped. Climbing and walking up the path towards the top where the water ran, I began to lose sight of the sky above me as the rift began to narrow. After a long walk, I could hear the splashing of the falls. I began to run, where my energy came from I can't imagine but I *actually* ran. That was when it happened.'

'What happened Scar, did you find water?' Nightfire asked.

'Not exactly, something found me. The first I knew was the loud dry rustling of wing feathers then I felt a strong tug around my shoulders. The flying death had miss-timed its attack, saving my back from its talons but it snagged my collecting bag instead. The great creature had dived deep into the rift and it hauled me up from the ground. For the first time in my life I was moving with no ground beneath my paws. It was not natural and really … *unpleasant*. I was thin and dry, less cat than I should have been or the creature would never have picked on me. Soon it had carried me up and out of the rift where it circled high above the ridge, gaining height as it flew. By this time, I just wanted it all to end. I actually hoped it would drop me. Then it turned towards Barren Moor and I feared the worst. I couldn't go through that again. If the flyer didn't kill me, I was sure the moor would. Then the beast circled again but this time it headed towards Greyfell Pike. I think its home was on the other side of the fell. Still with my collection bag firmly in its grip, the beast headed for the Pike but then the strangest thing happened. As I was being carried over the moor, the beast began to cry out as if others were challenging it for the food it carried.'

'Don't talk like that Scar. This tale is hard enough to hear without that thought in my head,' Becky complained.

'Sorry sis but this is the good bit, well sort of. The flying-death *was* fighting something but it was not another of its kind, crow or raven, it was old Ezra's protection spell. The shield charm he cast over the moor extended into the sky and the creature could feel it. As it fought to hang on to the collection bag and its next meal, the strap broke!'

'... And you fell! *That's* the good part! Scar, how ever did you survive the fall?' Becky was now close to tears.

'I don't really understand that bit but as I fell through the air and the ground rushed to meet me, I put my arms and legs out ready for the crash but that seemed to slow me down. I was thin, my skin hung loose on my bones, and as it caught the air my fall slowed. Oh, I still hit the moor with a thud that made me dark-sleep for hours but I was still in one piece and with nothing broken. When I woke, I was lying on a large soft bed of moss and wet to my skin but still me. I don't know why I didn't drink then, when I had the chance ... maybe I wasn't quite the me I used to be. Instead, I walked to another part of the moor where it was drier and lay in the sun to warm and dry out. I think I might have fallen asleep again. When I woke the next time it was much later and because of the way I had arrived, I had no idea where on the moor I was.'

'What did you do then?' Becky asked.

'I knew the direction the great sky-light travelled, and as it went down, I was able to see my course again. Then I headed towards the river on the far side of the moor. Once I reached the stream I knew that I could follow its bank back here, if I lasted that long. Anyway, with no predators to worry about on the moor I made good progress ... well if I am honest, *slow* progress. Something gnawed at my insides, and my legs grew tired and heavy, far more tired than they should have. I would have been easy prey in that state, had I still been on Barren Moor.'

'That was probably the effects of the spells and the stick-bite,' Nightfire replied.

'The last part of my journey felt like walking through great fields of snag-grass but there was something else slowing me down and that was the way I felt about being cast out by Silas. Do you realise that I am the first familiar to ever be banished, of course you do, and you're just too polite to say anything but I *was* banished!'

'Banished? He tried to *kill* you. That's a little more serious that firing you and sending you home,' Becky replied angrily.

'Whatever. I was the one that would have to live with the shame of it but then I realised it would not just be me. It would shame Leah, our mother. I did not know where to turn. I couldn't go home and I couldn't go back to Highfell. After that, I became mind-lost ... probably due to that bad frog. You know, I've really gone off frogs!' Scar laughed again, more for Becky's benefit as he could see how distressed she was becoming. 'I wandered without direction for some time. I struggled for hours with the half-thoughts that clogged my mind. I was lost, inside as well as on the moor. Then, somehow, I stumbled across the two of you but in my confused state, I didn't recognise your voices or your scent so again I hid. Well, as for the rest, you probably know that part of the tale better than I do ... I vaguely remember a horrible smell but nothing at all after that.'

'Sorry Scar, that was me,' Becky apologised sheepishly.

'Sis, what *had* you eaten?'

'No, it wasn't that, it was a potion!' Then she realised that her brother was regaining some of his cheek as well as his health. 'Besides, I only did it because we didn't know who or what *you* were at that point.'

'Thanks for being there for me, Fur-ball!' Scar replied softly.

'I'm Becky now, Uncle Nightfire named me.'

'What else could it have been, you always did have a fascination for water.'

'She still does!' Nightfire added. 'But what are we to do with you? You can't hide on the moors alone. Even on Highfell Moor, that's no life for a cat. You should return with us to the colony. When they know the whole story I'm sure they will understand.'

'Will they? I was there and even I don't understand what really happened. Where did Ethan go and what is wrong with Silas? No, there's no other way to look at it, I let the long line of Grimdyke wizards down ... badly. I was the one that left.'

'At least you are still alive *and* you returned to let us know that something is seriously wrong at Highfell. If we explain to the others that we have gained valuable information as a result of your return, they might just understand.'

'I can't help feeling that it would have been better if the flying-death had completed its task,' Scar sighed.

'Tomorrow we will face the colony together. Cheer up; facing your friends can't be any worse than what you've already been through,' Nightfire replied.

They settled down to an uneasy night on Greyfell Moor and tried hard not to think about what the morning might bring. During their sleep, visions of sky-death and weasels haunted Scar causing him to toss and turn repeatedly.

When morning finally came, they awoke to find they were not alone. Some of the older cats had sat up with them over night and a ring of senior cats had stood guard throughout the night as they slept.

Scar, Nightfire and Becky stretched and yawned themselves awake.

'We heard your fevered calls in the night and smelled the singed fur,' an old tom explained. 'A few of us decided that we should stand watch over you as you slept. It sounded like you needed the rest.'

'Thank you, Shadow, but now Scar must face the colony,' Nightfire explained.

'They will all be assembled now, Sure-foot called them together, earlier this morning. By now they will all be gathered in the old forge.'

'Oh great! I suppose I'd better get it over with,' Scar sighed.

'We'll go with you for support,' Becky and Nightfire agreed.

Slowly they walked the last short leg of the journey back to the forge. Nightfire, Scar and Becky being escorted by the older cats that had been on guard duty.

'If it is any consolation ...' an older female began, 'you would appear to have had little choice in the matter ... from what we overheard of your dream-mumblings.'

'Thanks ... I think,' Scar replied.

Minutes later, they faced the old force and the chattering coming from inside left Scar in no doubt that the colony already knew at least some part of his story.

'All in together, as one?' Nightfire asked.

'No, this is something I need to do alone,' Scar replied and took a deep breath before entering the building through the open doorway.

Once inside, gasps of shock ran around the old building. Scar was a mere shadow of his former self. As he reached the middle of the room, a deathly hush fell over the assembled group and Scar stood alone before his peers. Cats of all shapes, colours and sizes lined every surface. They sat on shelves, draped over roof beams, lay on old chairs and workbenches, in dry water troughs and on old anvils that had been left behind by the miners. Scar heard his mother Leah call to him but the elder cats were in charge of this meeting.

'You are the first! The first of our kind to return from the wizard's side before his time was up. What have you got to say?' The senior tom settled down to await Scar's answer.

Scar took a deep breath and began his story at the beginning with his surprise at finding Ethan gone, and going on to tell of the wizard's bog-grog fuelled temper leading Silas to try to kill him.

For one long hour, Scar related his attempts to work with Silas and how all his efforts to help had been rejected. He also told them of the protected sleep-box enchanted by Ethan, and how its magic had saved him from certain death. His description of his journey home had many of the cats visibly shaken and clearly impressed by his determination to return. Scar's story did not impress all that had gathered however. Some of the older ex-familiars thought that Scar should have shown the same determination to stay, rather that directing it towards getting him home.

Raven, who had been silent to this point, stood and asked to be heard. He explained how, while he was there, the old wizard had reluctantly handed over to Silas, both the keys of Highfell Croft and the responsibilities of the wizarding line, and how he had intended to warn Scar about the changes when he returned but to his shame, he failed.

'I too should have been more determined, more like you, Scar. I knew that you would face hard times with Silas but I let you go. I could have stunned you and made you listen but I didn't. I think I was hoping that you would succeed where I had failed. I thought I could turn Silas, I felt it was my duty to try. Ethan knew Silas had problems accepting his role as wizard but he clung to the hope that Silas would rise to the task and become a fine mage. It's not Scar's fault he returned early. If he had stayed, he would certainly be dead by now and at the end of seven years, we would have sent another chosen-one, this time Nappa, to replace him and to her certain death. It looks like our time with the Grimdyke wizards has come to an end and the real line actually ended years ago, with Ethan.'

Scar could see his mother, Leah in the crowd. She was glad to see him home safe but she knew what the others would say behind her back. She had been responsible for ending the colony's long relationship with the Grimdyke wizards and as a result, the valley would lose its protection.

'Maybe it's just as well. We have become soft. Scar has showed us what life is really about on the moors and who among us can truly say that they would have faired any better.' Nightfire raised a good point but one that just made them even more uncomfortable.

As the chatter around the old forge continued, senior cats and ex-familiars gathered to decide their verdict. Minutes later, after a long and heated discussion, they had decided. An old ginger female cat stepped forward.

'After hearing your account and considering how other ex-familiars see events, we have decided …'

'*I'm to be banished again, I can feel it!*' Scar thought as he waited for their verdict.

'… that Whitescar did all he could to support the Wizard Silas of Highfell. However some portion of blame must lay with his mother, Leah and his mentor here, Luna.'

The colony burst into a chattering, wailing explosion of complaints and hearty cheers in response to the decision.

A second cat from the group of elders then stepped forward.

'Another familiar must be dispatched immediately. The next chosen-one must replace the fallen Whitescar, regardless of the reception they may receive from this new wizard.'

'Nappa is too young!' Raven protested. 'Her training has hardly begun.'

'She *must* go, for the safety of the colony!' another, anonymous voice, called from the back of the room.

'I'll go!' a calm voice replied, oddly clear against the hubbub.

The room fell silent as the crowd tried to see who had spoken.

'I'll replace him. Scar is my brother and it is down to me to restore *both* family lines. The good names of Grimdyke and Leah-Long-night have been damaged by Silas and it is only right that I am allowed to set things right.'

Becky and Scar's parents were also charged with letting the down colony by providing a less than suitable familiar as replacement. Becky knew that the young Nappa was not yet ready and Raven and Luna too old to return for a second term. Scar was still far too weak to consider trying again and as far as Becky could see that left her as the only sensible choice.

'She is female and besides look at her size *or lack of it*. What can she do apart from make matters worse?' the elder female scoffed.

'I think you might be surprised, if you knew what this young cat can do!' Nightfire quietly announced in his usual restrained way and much to the annoyance of the elders. 'While your attention was on Whitescar and his training, this young female was learning at an astonishing rate. She has knowledge of creature-talk and can converse with many animal species on this moor. She has a mastery of potions that rivals either Raven's or my own but more than that, she has strength of will to match that of any tom in this colony. Furthermore, I too believe it is her right to be allowed to set straight her family's good name.'

'Your connection with Becky is well known and your indulging her with unofficial magical training has been endured by the elders but she is not the chosen-one!' the elder replied officiously.

'No, but right now she would be *my* chosen-one!'

'Does anyone else agree with Nightfire?' The elder reluctantly addressed the assembled colony. Slowly a yowl of agreement grew. Becky was amazed by how many supporters she had, even cats she had once thought of as strangers or even enemies, were now giving her their support. It then occurred to her that amongst the calls of support, there were probably a few that wanted her to fail or at least leave the colony permanently. As the cries died away, the elder called for any objectors to make their feelings known. The forge fell eerily silent. They were either too unsettled to show their disagreement or they had no better suggestion to offer. Becky chose to take this as a clear show of approval and left the forge. Luna, Raven, Scar and Nightfire followed. Once outside, in the still of the night, Becky stood alone, quietly looking over the distant moors.

'Regrets already Becky?' Nightfire asked.

'Only that it had to happen this way and that Scar had to face Silas alone.'

'I'm afraid, sis, there is one problem you may have overlooked. There is no trail for you to follow and without it you are lost before you even begin,' Scar reminded her.

'I will wait until first light and then ask the flyers which way I should travel, they will help me. I have friends amongst them from both moors. Between them, they must know the way to Highfell Croft.'

The four ex-familiars spent what remained of the day and some of the coming night, making sure that Becky was as prepared as she could be. Then they left her to get some much-needed sleep. As he too settled down, Scar was filled with an unsettling mix of concern and pride for his sister. Whatever Becky was thinking as she settled, she was keeping to herself.

CHAPTER ELEVEN
Leaving Home

At first light, Nightfire found Becky sitting on the old forge roof, staring across the moor. For once, he could not read her emotions as she prepared to face the unknown. Becky then shook herself and picked her way carefully down the crumbling stones of the smithy to meet Nightfire on the trackway bed.

'Are you sure you want to do this?'

'No … but I'm sure I *must*,' Becky calmly replied.

'If it is any comfort, you are the best *unofficial* familiar this colony has ever produced and although you were not originally chosen, we three, ex-familiars, have never before seen a more natural choice.'

Becky rubbed shoulders with her uncle before turning for Highfell. Whitescar, Raven and Luna lined the trackway leading out of the camp and as she passed them, they added their support and wishes for a safe journey and good stay with Silas.

'Remember to keep your head down sis,' Whitescar called.

'Don't go near the sour-water or the confoggating gas,' Raven added.

'Be safe,' Luna whispered, 'and come back in good health … *anytime*!'

Becky looked along the meandering line of the riverbank and into the distance. Somewhere ahead lay a turning point that would lead her onto the moor but where it was she could only guess. The trail left by Raven was now too old to follow and Whitescar had been too ill to lay a fresh one. Becky turned back one last time to see her friends still standing there and behind them, the rest of the colony. As she watched, Leah and Long-night stepped forward to sit with her uncle. It appeared that the whole colony had turned out to see her off and Becky secretly hoped that it would not be the last time she would see them.

'Ok Becks, time to put your money where your muzzle is. Don't let them see any fear or it will stay with them all the time you are away,' Becky prepared herself and then set out.

She could smell the water from the stream as she trotted along the riverbank. Then as a small twig joined her to float alongside in the water, she quickened her stride to keep up with it. Becky knew the moors well from her many foraging visits. However, it was the area upstream she knew the best and the further she followed the twig, the less familiar the landscape became to her. Some time into her journey, Becky slowed her pace again, she had left before eating and her stomach was now calling to her. Climbing carefully down the riverbank so that she could reach the stream, she watched as her only companion floated away, tripping over a small rapid before disappearing off into the distance. Becky walked along the water's edge until she came across a small pool. There she found food and drink, and ate her fill in preparation for the long trek across Greyfell Moor to Highfell Ridge.

'What I really need now are directions to the rift. It would take too long to climb over the peak and cause me to reveal my back to the flying-death. The moorland creatures here don't know me as well as the ones near to the forge but I really need their help right now.'

Becky found a small tree overhanging the stream and sitting a short distance away from it, she waited. She took care not to appear to be hiding and sat quite openly on the grassy bank, patiently waiting and watching.

'This could take some time.'

With a little time on her paws, Becky began a leisurely wash as she waited. Minutes later, a flash of bright blue darted across the waters, skimming the surface. Then just as quickly, it was gone again. This was followed by a splash in the pool after which the sparkling blue streak shot towards the nearby tree where it came to rest in its branches.

'Excuse me,' Becky said cautiously.

Startled, the kingfisher jumped, losing its grip on a small fish. After juggling with it in its beak for a moment, the bird finally got a better hold.

'Don't be nervous and please don't fly away.'

'You're talking!' the kingfisher replied through a mouthful of fish. 'You're not one of us so how is it you can talk … you're not having my fish if that's what you're thinking! Neither are you eating me, you're not fast enough!'

'I don't want to eat you or your fish. Actually, I need your help.'

The bird studied Becky thoughtfully for a minute.

'You're a … *cat*, aren't you?'

'*Oh, I found a smart one here!*' Becky sighed.

'No, I didn't quite catch that bit. You went back to meowing for a moment.'

'I need directions,' Becky insisted, 'and I was hoping you might be able to help.'

'No!'

'What do you mean "no"… is that all you have to say?'

'You could have the long answer if you prefer.'

'And what's that?'

'No way, four-legs, not in a thousand seasons.'

Becky turned to face the pool.

'Now what are you doing?' the kingfisher enquired.

Becky jumped, splashing water all over the bank.

'Wow. I've never seen anyone take "no" so badly before! Four-feet must have been more desperate than I thought.'

Becky then emerged from the water with two sticklebacks in her mouth, which she dropped at the foot of the small tree.

'You dropped them!' the kingfisher laughed, nearly dropping his own fish again.

'They're for you.'

'Why? I didn't help you.'

'No, but you might.'

The kingfisher looked first at the two small fish and then back to Becky. He then swallowed the fish he had in his beak before flying down and quickly scooping up the offering. Once safely back in the tree again, he turned to Becky.

'Alright, what do you want to know?'

'Well first, my name is Becky and I'm from the Greyfell Colony, upstream.'

'I'm Percival and I'm from a hole in the bank just over there.' The bird, still with the fish firmly clamped in its beak, nodded towards the far bank and a row of neatly excavated burrows dug into the soft peat.

'Now that we've been introduced and you know I'm not about to eat you, *can* you help me with some directions?'

Percival tipped his head to one side and eyed Becky suspiciously. 'I *do* know you, don't I? At least I've heard of you from my cousin, Rex. He lives upstream from here. He told me a tale about a strange four-legs that fed in the stream like he did. You must be Fur-splash!'

'Becky!'

'Bless you!'

'No, my name is Becky.'

'Well they call you Fur-splash upstream. I though he was pulling my wing when he told me. I mean, a four-legs, throwing itself into the water … it's not natural or I didn't think it was at the time.'

'Directions?' Becky persisted.

'Alright, ask me any question you like. I know every inch of this river inside out and wet side up. There's not a turn in this brook I don't know.'

'Do you know anything about the rift in the hill over there?'

'Why would you want to go there? There are no rivers there. Go on, ask me another.'

'I need to get to Highfell Croft and it's on the other side of that hill.'

'Persistent, aren't you. Well, there is a *very* small stream on the top, but no fish in it.'

'Could you at least show me where the stream is on the top?'

'You want a lot for your two fish, don't you, Fur-splash?'

'Alright, could you tell me where I should leave this river to head across the moor?'

Percival thought for a minute weighing the value of his gift.

'Alright, follow me … and *try* to keep up.'

Percival then downed the fish in one gulp before flying downstream pursued by Becky. Soon the bird was beginning to put distance between them and just as Becky was about to give up, she noticed a flash of blue in a nearby tree.

'Percival?'

'No, Cedric! Percival is over … hey, you can talk!'

'Oh no, not again! Where did you say Percival was?'

'O-o-over there in th-that tree. But you're … *talking*!'

'Anyone would think you've never seen a talking cat before.'

Becky ran to the next tree where she found another, identical kingfisher.

'Why were you talking to Cedric, he's no sense of direction that one,' Percival laughed.

'Is this where I should turn?'

'Turn, dance, flap your wings for all I care. I'm hungry again and you're on your own. Over there, on the top of the far hill, just where the ridge dips, that's where the water falls into a deep hole but it's too far for me to go and pointless anyway. Look, I know a feathered … er, *associate* who flies there, if I see him and I can persuade him to help, I'll ask him to meet you there.'

So saying, Percival darted away in a streak of brilliant blue.

'Daft creature!' Becky laughed.

Then she studied the ground around her feet for any signs of a trail. There was a slight shadow of something familiar, a distant memory of travellers past. Becky was certain she was on the right path.

'Maybe the blue-streak was being helpful after all.'

Becky looked back to the stream and before leaving for the unknown of the moors, she had something to eat and a good drink to set her on her way.

'I saw that!' a voice called. 'They're not all yours you know!' it was Percival. He was keeping an eye on Becky from further along the bank. Becky yowled back to him and again, Percival disappeared in sparkling flashes of blue, this time it appeared, for good.

'Right, this is it then girl. Time to see if their faith in you was well placed … it's also time to stop talking to yourself, Becks! Bad habit, Becky!'

Becky confidently leapt a nearby clump of heather and with the notch of the hillside firmly in her sights she set off across the moor. She knew that the entire journey could be completed in a day, if the trail was fresh and if the cat concerned was well fed but when there was no trail to follow ...

Becky followed the small runs left by other creatures that inhabited the moor. They wove in and out and across the moor between clumps of purple heather and thickets of ferns. Despite her best efforts, halfway across the moor, Becky lost sight of the notch in Highfell Ridge. She knew roughly the direction she should follow but without a proper trail, it could mean a lot of climbing. She also knew that this part of her journey would be the easy part. While she travelled Greyfell Moor, she would be under the protection of Ezra's spell but as Raven discovered, once outside the valley, it was every creature for itself.

Just then, Becky caught the scent of something dead or decaying on the breeze. She sniffed and then coughed. It was the confoggation gas of a nearby dark, dank bog. On either side of her stood stout banks of heather and fern, allowing no other way to go but straight on, towards the rank odour of death. Becky tried to leap the heather but she fell back onto the pathway. She had no better luck pushing her way through the stout stems of the bracken so she turned again to face the path ahead and pressed on. The narrow trail then started to dip and the grass beneath her paws began to squelch under her step. The water was bitter smelling and Becky had to fight hard to resist the urge to lick her paws clean. Trying to hold her breath was not working and so she quickened her step to get away from the smell and the danger as fast as she could.

Turn followed bend and twist followed narrow, until finally she was confronted by a broad bubbling expanse of dark water. As her head began to spin from the effects of the marsh gas, Becky understood the dangers that came from delaying in these parts of the moor. Carefully she began to edge her way around the pool, the oily film on the pond's surface swirling about her feet as she walked. Becky could see the pathway on the opposite side of the bog but why was it swaying like that? She shook her head and picked up the pace. Minutes later, she had made it.

On dry ground again, but still light-headed, Becky looked for clean water so that she could drink and rid herself of the foul smell that now clung to her coat. As she walked, the ground beneath her paws began to feel dry again and her head clearer and then finally came the smell of sweet water. Around the next turn, a small spring rose on the moor, creating a head of water that trickled into the moor to feed its pools and bogs, but at its source it was the sweetest water in the whole fell. As Becky approached, she heard splashing. She immediately sank down low and without disturbing a single stem or making the slightest sound, she began slipping through the reed and heather beds. Eventually she could see the pool and its happy visitor, the cause of the disturbance. Splashing about and revelling in the water was a kingfisher. For the moment, it was completely unaware of her presence and contentedly preening and washing its brightly coloured feathers.

'Cedric?'

'Don't you know it's rude to spy on a chap when he's in the bath! Besides, it's, Percival. You four-legs have poor eyesight, don't you? You're lucky you made it this far.'

'I thought you said I'd be on my own for the rest of the way?' Becky smiled.

'Well it's not everyday a four-legs asks for directions, is it?' Percival replied cheekily. 'Besides, I had a word with Beaky and he said he would fly over the water so that you could see where it was but he won't be there all evening so you'd better get going. Hey, I've just realised, Becky – Beaky, Beaky – Becky you have nearly the same names.'

'And I thought you couldn't remember mine.'

Before she left, Becky stepped into the water to wash at which point Percival took off like a rocket, to come to rest on a small stunted tree a few feet away.

'Hey, we've only just met and you want to share a bath! That's not the way we do it round these parts, Fur-splash!'

Becky ignored the priggish bird's complaints and carried on washing. Then after finding the point at which the clear water burbled its way to the surface, she had a long drink in preparation for the next leg of her journey.

'Thanks!' Becky called to the bird.

'What for, stealing my bathwater!'

'No, for caring enough to see if I made it this far.'

'Oh, well it's not every day you get to meet a talking cat!'

Becky shook off the last of the water from her coat and resumed her journey.

'So far, so good. Now where is the other bird Percival talked about?'

Circling the ridge high above her was a young buzzard, lazily gliding around on the evening thermals. A simple task for someone of his flying skills, and as a favour to a friend it was little more than he would normally do on a warm evening. As she watched this master of the air and one of the less troublesome of the flying-death, Becky was amazed at the way it could leave the circling flight of the thermal and hover over the moor, watching as it sought out its prey. Suddenly, the hover came to an end and the bird dived towards the ground below.'

'I hope that wasn't someone I knew,' Becky wondered, uncomfortably.

Moments later the buzzard took to the air again, its talons empty. Unusually for Beaky, he had miss-timed the strike and his would-be snack had eluded him.

'Percival has some strange friends,' Becky thought as she watched her new guide in action. 'Buzzards can be a bit ...

snappy sometimes but they do have good eyes. If he's showing me the cleft in the hill where the water runs in, all I need to do now is find the entrance.'

A simple thing or so Becky thought but the bleached white, craggy stones of the ridge gave little away to the casual visitor and the entrance to the pass was well hidden. Becky searched and searched but without a clear scent trail to follow it proved to be an impossible task. As time passed, the buzzard tired of waiting and it left the ridge in search of food. Becky climbed up onto a large rock and sat down to think.

'What now Becks? There's no going back to the colony and no clear way forward. Back at the forge, it seemed like the right thing to do at the time … it *is* the right thing to do but I can't climb the ridge it's far too high. Come on think … think … *and* you're still talking to yourself!'

Becky stood up again and scanned the area for clues but then, at the base of the boulder, something distracted her. Running around the rock, completely unaware of her presence, was a small rat.

'Excuse me!'

'Eh, who said that? Your accent is strange. You're not from around here are you?'

'Don't run away, I'm coming down,' Becky called to the startled rat.

Hoping not to frighten the traveller rodent, she carefully climbed down off the rock rather than jumping and soon she stood on the pathway behind him. She dismounted so quietly in fact that he remained unaware of her arrival.

'Show yourself, I may be small but there are few rats that can best me in a fight!'

'I'm not here to fight!' Becky replied quietly.

The small rat immediately jumped and then turned around to face Becky.

'You're not a rat either!' he screamed before scuttling for cover in a nearby bank of heather. 'You don't scare me!' he added defiantly if a little unconvincingly from inside the shrub.

'I should!' Becky replied. 'You won't last long trusting every cat you meet.'

'Cat, eh? So you're *not* just a big rat then?'

'Not really. I'm Becky, from the Greyfell Colony.'

'I'm petrified, from a hole just over there,' a small pink paw pointed shakily through a gap in the heather. 'But you're talking *rattish*! That's not right! How is that possible if you're *not* a rat? Are you absolutely sure you're not just overweight?'

'I don't think so but as for the talking rattish bit, I've never stopped to think about it.'

'Do you ever stop to think how hungry you are?' the rat then asked nervously.

'Frequently, but I only eat fish so you're quite safe with me.'

A sharply pointed nose twitched cautiously through the stems of heather, followed by a set of equally twitchy whiskers and then a pair of bright, bead-like black eyes. For a moment, the rat just stared at Becky. Then it pushed through the tangle of stems to stand on the pathway. Still with one eye on its escape route, the rat addressed Becky again.

'Why would a clawpaw like you want to talk rattish?' But just as suddenly as it had surfaced, bravery appeared to abandon him again and he darted back inside the heather.

'I'm trying to find the way through the hillside.'

'Why?' the rat's muffled voice enquired. 'What's on the other side that would interest a clawpaw?'

'I need to reach Highfell Croft, home of the Wizard Grimdyke.'

'Grimdyke?' the rat appeared to be familiar with the name. 'They've gone bad, the Grimdykes. They chased us from the moor, not that we minded leaving there, it was a naff place anyway. Why would *you* want to … 'ere, you're not a milliar are you?'

'If you mean *familiar*, no, not exactly but I'm hoping to set things right with Silas, the new wizard.'

'Good luck to you! My friend Norman …'

'… *Norman*?'

'Yes, what's wrong with Norman?'

'Nothing,' Becky smiled. 'What about Norman?'

The rat ground his teeth and even appeared to growl at Becky for her remark.

'*Norman* was in the croft one night, just trying to keep warm nothing else … well, apart from collecting a bit of chocolate … oh and a piece of cake, that's all … nothing else. Anyway, after taking a sip of bog-grog and a …'

'I don't want to rush you but could you get to the point.'

'The point is,' the rat replied decidedly, 'that Norman wasn't doing anything apart from …'

'… Warming his toes and filling his face?'

'… Well, a bit! Anyway, in comes Silas just as Norman has got the lid off a big tin of sweets and then … he blasts him, just like that, for nothing!'

'Did he … was Norman … *dead*?'

'Nah, Silas is a rotten shot and he missed, well, he *nearly* missed. He blew Norman's tail clean off his bum!'

'That was lucky.'

'Lucky, LUCKY you call it. Norman now looks like a hamster! What sort of look is that for a street-smart rat?'

'Well he could have blown up Norman, then all you'd have left would be his whiskers!'

'Good point, good point. Ok, so it's been ten minutes and you haven't tried to eat me, I suppose that proves something. Anyway I'm full of diseases and I'd make you ill if you took even the smallest bite out of me.'

'Really?'

140

'No, not really but we rats always give it a try when someone is thinking about eating us! It usually puts them off. *Anyway* ... I'm Rodney and before you ask, no, not the guy from the film on the telly! Although I have been told that I look like him.' The rat licked a finger and smoothed down an eyebrow.

'What's a "*telly*" or "*film*" for that matter?'

'You don't get in much, do you? He's a character in fi ... oh, forget it. Let's start again. I'm Rodney.'

'I'm Becky, pleased to meet you.'

'Becky? ... Becky! Why didn't you say so in the first place? I have an uncle whose paw you fixed. He got a bad swelling from a thorn and you fixed it for him with a pot-on.'

'Potion ... it's pronounced, potion,' Becky corrected him.

'Yeah, like your rattish couldn't stand some improvement!'

'Sorry, but about my little problem ...'

'Yeah, you wanted directions through the hill to Highfell Croft, right?'

'There's a rift, a pathway through the hillside to Barren Moor but I can't find the entrance.'

'A pathway through the hill ... you mean the long burrow. That's easy, we use it when we come and go between moors.'

'Can you show me where it is?'

'Are you sure you want to go through it? It's dark, wet and very long.'

'It doesn't sound quite right but it must be the way.'

'There's no food in there ...'

'I know. I'll eat before I go in.'

'You did say you only ate fish?' Rodney checked again.

'Yes, I told you, you're quite safe.'

'Ok then ... it's your neck.' Rodney turned and ran away down the trail where he paused and called back, 'Try to keep up!'

This time it was a little easier for Becky. The rat was fast, very fast for his size but as Becky trotted after him, she found it easy to keep up. Gradually the ground began to rise and the wetness of the moor gave way to stone and scree. Scrambling over the blanket of loose rock, Becky noticed that Rodney was beginning to tire.

'Look I wouldn't normally say this but … if it helps, you can ride on my back and I'll carry you. Then you can point the way.'

Rodney looked up at Becky and thought for a moment, and then he called:

'Hey, we'll be just like Remy in Rata … oh, never mind. I forgot for a moment that you don't watch much television.' Rodney climbed up the spine of a stout fern and then jumped onto Becky's back where he settled down for the ride. 'Giddy-up!' he rashly called out.

'Don't push it! And if anyone asks, you're my packed lunch!'

Rodney gulped but then he could feel Becky laughing beneath him.

'Oh very funny. Yeah you fooled the rat … cat humour, *really*!'

Becky and her nervous passenger climbed the scree slopes together with ease and, as Rodney called out directions, Becky made good progress.

'Hey, Clawpaw, I think I've just invented Rat-nav!' Rodney chuckled, then he realised, 'Never mind, you'll see how funny that was when the wizard is called to fix another broken sat-nav, then you'll see how funny rat-humour is. That is if anyone ever talks to the wizard again!'

Minutes later, they reached a small stream running down the side of the hill and Becky stopped to sniff the water.

'Hey, don't drink that!' Rodney called out and he tugged on the fur on Becky's neck.

'Ow! Now what's wrong, I just thought it didn't smell right, that's all.'

'You're right. One of my mates drank some of that once.'

'What happened, did he die?'

'No, but it changed him. We rats are tough, you know, but ... well let's just say he's not called Brains anymore, his name now is Dingle-rat, and leave it at that. Just remember, nothing lives in this water, no fish, no weeds ... *nothing*. So even we leave it alone now. Come on, it's not far. This way.'

They headed upstream, following the crystal-clear waters as they went but Becky could not help thinking, that wherever this was leading, it did not sound much like the pass she was seeking. She knew the water that ran there was sweet and safe to drink, so where were they headed now? Minutes later, she had her answer, at least part of it. At the head of the stream, they found a neatly arched hole that lead into the hillside. Even to Becky's eyes, it did not look natural and it was definitely not the rift she was seeking. Set around the opening, the stones were neatly arranged and something about the appearance reminded her of the smithy and the old mine workings near to her old home.

'We think humans made this a long time ago,' Rodney explained with great authority. 'Either that or *really* big rats! Friends that have been in the houses of Skellside have seen drawings of this run. They say it was dug so that humans could bring rocks through the hillside to the village. Yes, I know, that's what I thought, it sounds mad. What would anyone want with rocks ... but that's what they said all right. All I know is that this run goes straight through the hill to Barren Moor on the other side but it is foodless and full of bad water, not the sort of place to get lost or delay. Look, if you're serious about going in there, you had better take this.'

Rodney handed Becky a small stick.

'What's this, some sort of dried food?'

143

'What? No, it's Norman's tail!'

'EEUW!' Becky cried, immediately dropping the stick-like offering.

Rodney picked it up and carefully dusted it off again.

'Norman thought it might be possible to reattach it somehow but the longer we took to work out how, the drier and more shrivelled the tail got. Now we just keep it to show we are friends of Norman or part of the "Brotherhood of the tail" as we like to call ourselves.' Rodney then coughed and appeared to snap-out of his nostalgic thoughts. 'If you need help, just show it to any rat and they will know you are one of us … well, you know what I mean.'

'Thank you, I'll make sure it gets back to you.'

'If you begin to feel lost or alone, here's something else for you to think about. Did you know, that wherever we rats gather, we're never any more than ten feet from a human? Yeah, crazy I know but they seem to get everywhere!' Rodney then jumped to the ground. 'Let me know how you get on with the wizard and … mind out for your tail.'

CHAPTER TWELVE
Tunnel Collapse

Becky said goodbye to Rodney and turned to face the forbidding tunnel entrance.

'A talking cat! Wait till the others hear about this!' Rodney laughed to himself.

The stream that ran from out of the mine level looked inviting but it smelled all wrong. Even the tunnel itself was dark and threatening and the air that drifted out of its mouth was damp and had an odour of bog-gas about it, and strangely of Rodney too for some reason. Becky took a deep breath of the cleaner air outside before stepping into the tunnel.

For the first few moments, she could see nothing but as her sensitive eyes grew more accustomed to the gloom, she began to make out shapes and even the distant glimmer of light at the other end of the tunnel. The mine level was indeed a route through to the far side of the ridge and it had been dug in a dead straight line, if not perfectly flat. As Becky started to walk, her paws could detect a slight gradient in her route. The way into the mine led slightly up hill. This grade was the mine engineer's solution to clearing the water that seeped into the tunnel from the many fissures and watercourses.

Now better adjusted to the darkness, Becky set off at a brisk pace, trotting along the old iron cart-rails that had been left behind. However, before she had gone more than a few metres, she saw something glinting in the dark. Something on the floor was reflecting the light that shone in behind her; also, she noticed that the smell of Rodney was growing stronger.

Becky sank down into her stalking position and proceeded more cautiously into the tunnel.

'Stop! Whoever you are come fo nurther, I mean, no further!' It was a small rattish voice, which sounded very much like her earlier guide. 'I have a cocktail stick and I'm not afraid to use it.'

'I'm sorry,' Becky replied, 'I don't have any cheese for you to put on it.'

'Who are you, your accent is strange.'

'I know, I get that a lot.'

'Come closer brother and show yourself,' the rat urged.

Becky walked slowly into the tunnel in the direction of the small voice and suddenly the rat realised his mistake.

'Traps and whippets! It was all a trick. You're no rat at all; you're one of those clawpaw creatures. *You're also on your own.*' The rat began gathering up his belongings ready to flee. Bits of silver paper, plastic and bracken were all hurriedly scooped up in preparation for retreat.

'I was led here by Rodney; he's a member of the Brotherhood of the tail.' Becky paused to see if it meant anything to the rat.

'If you know about the Brotherhood, then you must know about … the sacred twigglet.'

Becky thought for a moment.

'Oh, you mean this?' Becky held out the dried remains of Norman's tail.

'The sacred twigglet!' the rat repeated again respectfully.

'You wouldn't happen to be Dingle-rat, by any chance?'

'Why would you say that?'

'Oh, there's just something about you that rang a bell.'

'So you hear them too! They said I was crazy hearing bells all the time but don't you worry, you're as sane as I am. They said, Dingle, he's a sandwich short of a picnic, that one.'

'Sandwich, picnic … what are they?'

146

'You don't get *in* much, do you?'

'No, I get *that* a lot too. Are they anything to do with humans?'

'Yeah, it's something they do before they can eat. Strange creatures of habit, humans. They wrap all their food into little packets and then leave their homes to travel miles before eating it. What they do makes no sense at all. Oh, I'm Dingle-rat, pleased to meet you … no don't come any closer. You may carry the sacred twigglet but how do I know you didn't eat Rodney to get it?'

'Good point, I guess you'll just have to trust me on that.'

'Anyway, what's a clawpaw doing in here? Only we rats travel the long burrow. You're bit off your normal hunting ground aren't you?'

'I'm trying to get to Highfell Croft. Rodney told me that this burrow leads straight to Barren Moor.'

'There's nothing there but trouble and now there's a mad wizard in charge it's even less attractive! But you're right; it does lead to the moor … for now at least.'

'What do you mean?'

'The long burrow is old and pieces of it keep falling from the roof.'

'Well I have no choice. I have to get to Highfell Croft, to set things right with Silas.'

'Good luck with him. I hope your tail is screwed on or he'll blast it off like Norman's.'

'I'd better get going. If you see Rodney, give him this and say "thanks", for me.' Becky then handed Dingle-rat the withered tail and set off down the tunnel.

'And they call me mad … Ah, the sacred twigglet! Wait! Before you go I should give you something in return, it's the rat code. Take this sleeping tube. I found it on the moor. It had a broken loop on it but I fixed it. Now there's no cause to look like that, I haven't slept in it yet! Right now all that's left is to say bud guy … I mean good bye.'

Becky took the long plastic tube and looked closely at it. Then it occurred to her that it could be the collecting bag that April had made for Whitescar.

'Thank you, this means a lot to me.'

She passed her head through the loop and set off again for the light at the far end of the tunnel. Bravely Becky trotted deeper into the darkness with only thoughts of helping Silas to encourage her. Minutes passed, until finally, there was a subtle change when the rail she was walking on began to level out and she could hear the steady drip and splash of water.

'This must be the half-way point. The water falling in the pass above must have found its way into this burrow.'

Just ahead, water was indeed pouring into the tunnel and the noise echoed to her down the roughly hewn walls, as they amplified the sound.

'I wonder if it's safe to drink? Better not risk it.'

All of a sudden, there was a rumble then a roar of destruction as the water-worn boulders of the tunnel roof slipped and crashed to the floor. As they fell on the metal track rails, the ground shook violently beneath her paws. One of the smaller rocks then hit the bag on Becky's back knocking her to the ground where she lay, dazed in the dark. How long she had lain there, she had no idea but when she came to, she was cold and very wet.

'Clawpaw? … Clawpaw! Is you alive?'

'No!' Becky replied and for a moment, she could almost believe it herself.

'Oh, I's too late, Cloor pawpaw … I mean, poor Clawpaw!'

'What happened?' Becky asked as she struggled to her feet again.

'Well, before you died, the burrow roof must have collapsed and squished you.'

'I'm not really dead, Dingle; at least I don't think I am but what do I do now?'

'Come out, I suppose. This is a big burrow-fall, biggest I's ever seen.'

'But I still need to get to Barren Moor.'

'You say that a lot for a dead rat!'

'Well it's important.'

'I suppose I *could* try sniffing out a way through … *if* there is one.'

Dingle-rat then set about climbing and snuffling in the rubble. Occasionally he would disappear for a moment only to return moments later to shout 'dead-end' to Becky. Minutes gradually ticked by and Becky began to despair. Then Dingle reappeared again.

'Found it! I bumped into Ruby coming the other way.' Then he lowered his voice and whispered, 'Don't stare when you see her, she's not like us. She used to be a pet in one of the Skelside cottages but we broke her out a year ago and she's been with us ever since.'

Just then, a grubby looking white nose appeared amongst the rubble followed by two beady red eyes.

'Strewth Dingle, your new friend's one *big* rat! If I didn't know better I'd have said that was a C-A-T!'

'I don't want to worry you, Rube but sometimes she actually thinks she is,' Dingle replied. 'If she is, she speaks pretty good rattish for a c-a-t. Anyway she's a little mixed up so don't say anything about it,' Dingle explained to the white rat.

'I'm Becky pleased to meet you.'

'Did she just say pleased to *eat* me?'

'No, relax, Ruby. Beaky knows Rodney.'

'It's Becky!' Becky corrected, but Ruby ignored her as instructed.

'Are you telling me this clawpaw knows the brotherhood and speaks rattish?'

'Yeah, sort of … she's got the strangest accent though,' Dingle replied.

'Do you think the hole is big enough for me to get through?' Becky asked, in an attempt to steer the conversation back to the problem at hand.

'Good chance, although I wasn't allowing for quite such a big er, rat,' Ruby replied tactfully.

'I'm a c-a-t,' Becky replied, 'and as far as my kind go, I'm a fairly small example or so my brother tells me.'

'Your brother? You have a brother? Wait, does he look a lot like you but even bigger!'

'That's Scar alright and we're the same in every detail, even down to the moon on our chests … apart from the difference in our size, that is.'

'He's enormous! I heard that posh cat, Sebastian, talking about him one day. He said Scar was huge,' Ruby explained to Dingle, 'but he reckoned he was Ok … for an outdoors cat. He also said Scar was milliar to the wizard.'

'Look, can we get back to finding a way out.'

'Yeah, it should be no trouble for a big rat like you … follow me.'

Ruby then turned and disappeared into the jumble of boulders that lay blocking the tunnel.

'*I think they should all be called Dingle*!' Becky muttered.

'This way, c-a-t … *daft rat*!' Dingle called to her. 'I scented the trail so it should be easy to follow.'

'Oh goody!' Becky thought. 'More rat pee!'

As she squeezed into the gap between the boulders, smaller stones continued to fall from the roof after which they would roll down the tunnel-collapse and onto the floor. The going was very tight but passable, with a little effort. It wasn't long before Becky was forced to hold the collecting bag in her teeth, pushing it in front of her as she scrabbled through the rock fall. Every few minutes either Dingle or Ruby would return to her to see how she was getting on.

'You know, you could probably stand to lose a few pounds. A rat shouldn't let her figure go like that,' Ruby commented. 'You could try the "Ratkins Diet". It worked for me. Oh and get your owner to buy you an exercise wheel, they're great. You might tell them to get you one of the *larger* wheels. A rat's got to look after her figure.'

'C-A-T!' Becky repeated.

'Right, O-k! ... Hey Dingle, you're right, she's convinced she's a cat. Drunk much of the water has she?'

Progress was slow but the encouraging words of her two guides kept Becky going. By the time she had finally cleared the roof-fall, Becky was filthy and in desperate need of a good wash. She also smelled a little too strongly of rat.

'NO, STOP! You can't do that. That's bad water that is and the mud in here is worse still. Licking that off your fur would kill you in days.' Dingle stopped her just in time.

'Thanks Dingle but I can't stay like this.'

'Look, the way is clear from here and just before you leave the burrow you will find another forter-wall ... I mean, water-fall. There the water is better and you can wash in it safely ... well, at least it's not too bad. Just don't drink it. If you want to drink, wait until you are outside again. Around the burrow entrance on Barren side, you'll find some prick-nose plants. They always have lots of water in them. Right, if that's everything, we've got to go the other way now. Be careful c-a-t Becky, we don't want to lose any more good rat tails to Silas' bad magic.'

Dingle and Ruby then disappeared into the jumble of rocks and were gone, leaving Becky alone in the tunnel. Becky turned to face the light coming from the exit and trying hard to ignore her natural instinct to wash, she followed the metal rail towards fresh air and the way out. Minutes later, just as Dingle had predicted, she found running water. A much smaller stream than before was running through the tunnel roof providing a perfect shower in which Becky could finally wash. After washing off the last of the mud and dirt from her fur, she stepped clear of the water and shook herself dry.

'Now what I need is some warm sun … and a drink!'

With the exit in sight, Becky began to run and soon she could smell warm dry air and the scent of heather. Minutes later, she stood in the tunnel exit, blinking in the bright light. She had made it, and in one piece but then she got her first view of Barren Moor and her relief quickly turned to despair as she surveyed the dismal sight below. Becky sank slowly to the ground. This moor was a terribly bleak place. It was dreary, almost uniformly brown and completely uninviting. Then she remembered that unlike Greyfell, this moor also held an additional terror. This place had no protection charm and every creature that called it home, fought with every other for food and shelter.

It was at this point that Becky realised that her real adventure had yet to start.

CHAPTER THIRTEEN
The Un-familiar Cat

'Right, first things first. I wonder what a "prick-nose" plant looks like. I could *really* use a drink now.'

Becky studied the area around the mine entrance and the rocks along the foot of the ridge. Here and there tall, lush green towers stood proud above the stubby grass. These lofty spires of green bore long, wrinkled leaves that met in pairs at the single, stout stem. Becky went closer to investigate.

'Hey, this is my prick-nose, clear off!' a small voice warned bravely from behind the teasle.

'Well that's charming,' Becky replied. 'Is that how you greet all visitors to this moor?'

'Why would anyone visit *this* moor, besides, it doesn't take a genius to work out that you're a clawpaw!'

'You're a bit quicker than the other two rats I met in the long-burrow.'

'What other two ... did you *eat* them?'

'Certainly not! They helped me to find a way out.'

'A rat helped a clawpaw ... that sounds unlikely ... unless it was Dingle-rat. He's the only one barmy enough to help one of *your* kind,' the rat replied dismissively. 'Who was the other rat?'

'She was called Ruby.'

'Hah! Another nut job. She used to be a pet! Imagine living in a cage with humans and them on the outside of it. It's just not natural. After her time with them she thinks she understands humans *and* cats ... here ... you're talking rattish!'

'Not *that* quick are you?'

'But clawpaws don't talk, they just catch and eat. Why do you think we call you clawpaws ... the clue is in the name, *durr*!' The rat then darted behind the thick spiky stem of the prick-nose, and hid.

'I know this is a bad place, everyone for himself and all that but I'm from the Greyfell Colony and ...'

'... You're not Fur-splash are you? I've heard about you. They reckon you talk to other animals,' the rat spluttered into a fit of giggles. '*And we thought Dingle was crazy*,' the rat muttered.

'You mean like I'm talking to you right now?'

'Yeah ... oh, I see what you mean. You're not all that daft then, are you?'

'I try not to be. My name is Becky and you are?'

'Me? I'm not sure but I think I might be your dinner.'

'You have my word, I won't eat you, besides you're full of disease aren't you?' Becky smiled.

'Yeah and don't you forget it ... wait a minute, you've been talking to Rodney, haven't you?'

'We did have a little chat.'

'And how did *he* taste?' the rat asked accusingly, still not entirely convinced that his name wasn't on the menu.

'Rodney is fine and so too are Ruby and Dingle so why don't you come from behind the plant and introduce yourself properly.'

The rat poked a small leaf around the side of the stem to see if Becky would pounce and much to his surprise and relief, nothing happened. He then peered at her from the cover of a large drooping leaf.

'Not hungry, eh?'

'Not for rats. I only eat fish.'

'Oh yeah, I remember now. That's why they call you Fur-splash, because you're always in the water catching fish. Ok, I'm coming out but just you stay where I can see you. I've got a cocktail stick ...'

'... And you're not afraid to use it, yes, I know. Dingle challenged me the same way.'

'So you really did meet old Dingle.'

'Yes. He seemed nice, if a little confused.'

'He's a good guy but he drank too much in the long-burrow. He used to be a genius that one but now ...'

As his bravery returned a little, the rat emerged from behind the tall plant.

'You must be Norman! I recognise the ... well, the lack of ...'

'Yes! Got something to say have you, Clawpaw?'

'Well it's just that ... I think I've been carrying your tail with me through the tunnel.'

'Rodney trusted you with that did he? Maybe you are alright after all.'

'Look, to show you that there's nothing to fear from me, let me do something for you.'

Becky dashed down the slope and began gathering plants in the collection bag. Some minutes later she returned, much to Norman's surprise.'

'I thought you'd just leg-it when you got the chance. There aren't many that would challenge a fighting rat armed with a cocktail stick.'

Becky emptied the leaves she had collected onto a large flat stone and began to grind them into a paste with the aid of another, smaller flat pebble.

'This is really a little too dry but it should still work.'

'You could use some of the water from this prick-nose.' Realising what he had said, Norman suddenly and clamped a paw over his mouth. 'Drat, I was going to keep that a secret!'

'So this is the famous prick-nose.'

'Yes, water collects in it around the stem at the bottom of the leaves. If you get there before the flies drown it or the frogs claim it as "*their pond*", daft creatures, then you can drink the water. It's clean and sweet and the safest source of water around here. Here, I wasn't going to tell you *any* of that! Are you a witch or something, did you cast a blabbering spell on me?'

'No, I think that was all you. And I'm not a witch but I hope to be a familiar one day.'

'A milliar? Not to Silas Grimdyke, he's the one ...'

'... I know, he's the one that blasted your tail clean off your bum!'

'You *did* meet Rodney. He always tells that story.'

Becky walked towards Norman and the prick-nose plant. Norman stood his ground for all of two seconds before thinking better of it and retreating to the safety of the bracken. From a safe distance, he then watched as Becky tried to lap water from the small cauldron shaped bowls at the base of the leaves.

'OW! I can see now why you call this "prick-nose". Every bit of it is covered with sharp spikes.'

Norman sniggered at her poor performance but Becky was not beaten yet. Carefully she placed a paw on the largest leaf at the bottom of the plant. Then, by pushing it down and out of the way, she could get her head near enough to the water to drink without pricking her nose on the barbs.

'Hum, not so daft after all!' Norman admitted as he watched.

Becky smiled at him then drank some of the water. Then she took an extra large lap at the small pool and carried some of the water to the crushed leaves. There she wetted the pulp and it began to fizz.

'Oh, that's nice, dribble on the food why don't you, and they say rats have bad manners!'

'This isn't food, it's a potion,' Becky explained.

'I think you'll find it's pronounced *pot-on*!' Norman corrected.

'What is it with rats! Look, whatever it's called this *pot-on* is for you.'

'Why, I'm not ill but I will be if I eat that … *mush*!'

'It's a poultice, and it's not for eating.'

'*Pull-tice*? Where do you expect me to stick that then?'

'Well …' Becky grinned. 'It's to help your tail re-grow so I suppose you'd better stick it …'

'No – way Clawpaw! I may look like an oversized hamster to you but I still have some dignity left!'

'But no tail,' Becky reminded him and then she waited while Norman struggled to find a suitable put-down.

'Let me get this straight. I, a rat of some distinction and notoriety I might say, I'm supposed to let you, a clawpaw, shove that … that *mush* up my …'

'… *Dab* some of it *onto* your rear end!' Becky quickly corrected him.

'Oh, that's alright then … what am I saying! It's still sounds like tap-dancing in a blender to me!'

'What's a blender … or tap-dancing for that matter? … Never mind, I already know, "I don't get in much!" I have been told before.'

'How would it be if I rubbed it on myself?'

'Fine, but just make sure you wash your paws after or you'll grow extra thumbs.'

'Wash? WASH! Look, I don't mind having green mush shoved up my …'

'… *ON* your tail …' Becky interrupted again.

'… but if you think I'm having a wash … forget it! I'm a rat. We have certain standards to uphold.'

'Right, I forgot,' Becky replied as she tried hard to hide a giggle.

'Just stay there where I can see you and stay away from the mush *and* my bottom!'

With one eye firmly fixed on Becky and the other on the leaf pulp, Norman edged slowly towards it. Cautiously he then climbed on top of the rock where he sniffed the mush.

'Few-wee! Are you *sure* this will work?'

'Get on with it. I have to be at the Croft before dark!'

Norman then began to rub the stumpy remains of his tail into the leaf pulp.

'It tingles!' he complained. 'And now it's getting hot! Is it supposed to do that?'

'Just give it time to work,' Becky replied calmly.

'Something's happening!' Norman stopped rubbing and turned round to look at his green rear-end. 'It's actually working!'

As the tingle grew so too did Norman's tail. He was ecstatic. He danced around, jumped and cheered. 'A tail, I've got my tail back!' Unfortunately, his energetic display drew the attention of a large hawk that had been circling overhead. It swooped down to grab a bite to eat but luckily, Norman spotted it.

'Er, must dash … this is brilliant. Thanks Clawpaw, I mean *Becky* … got to go! It would be a shame to lose the tail again, to a hawk!'

Norman dived for cover into a thicket of bracken just seconds before the hawk crashed into the teasel, getting a good soaking and a face full of prickles but no snack.

'Well, that's not the sort of language I expect to hear from a big bird like you!' Becky commented to the hawk.

The hawk grumbled some more before flying away, empty handed and as the bird flew away into the distance, Norman reappeared.

'Highfell Croft is over there. Just follow the track and a smell of burning peat; you can't miss it. Take my advice though, don't go in but if you do, you had better have a good supply of this green mush ... you'll need it!'

Becky thanked Norman and set off for the croft. As she neared the end of her journey, the evening light began to fade. Soon the sun would set and she would face the wizard that tried to kill her brother. What was she to do?

'Attack first and hope to end the long line of Grimdyke wizards before Silas ruins the good name?' No, that was not her way. 'Plead with him to take Scar back?' Pleading was not her style either and Scar had no intention of returning to Highfell. 'I guess I'll have to play it by ear and hope my tail stays where it is supposed to be.'

Around the next turn in the small track, Becky could see the croft and the smoke rising from its chimney. She stood outside the small garden gate and peered through the slats to the lighted windows of the cottage.

'No point in staying out here Becks; you have a job to do.'

Becky leapt onto the drystone wall of the cottage garden and then down onto the path inside that led to the front door.

Once inside the garden she quickly picked up Scar's tracks, which she followed to the rear of the croft. Confronted by the cat flap, she sniffed cautiously at the air and then the small door.

'This is the place alright. Nothing else for it but to go in.'

While Becky had been gathering the ingredients for Norman's tail-potion, she took the precaution of collecting what she would need to make a protection charm. The spell would be small and short lasting but if called upon, it would shield her if she needed to make a hasty retreat.

Becky pushed open the flap and with the potion in her other paw, she stepped inside. Silas heard the flap creak and fearing the rats had come back, he withdrew his wand and approached the kitchen. Becky and Silas met halfway across the kitchen floor, with Becky standing in the small crater that Silas had created when he had tried to evaporate Scar.

'T-this … isn't … p-possible!'

Silas stammered and the wand in his hand trembled and fell. Just days earlier, he had oblivorated his old familiar, yet there he now stood, intact and perfectly healthy. Silas first looked at his empty wand-hand and then to his rejuvenated familiar.

'Jet black … the small crescent moon in white … the collecting bag he always carried! He's returned! He must be *far* more powerful than I ever gave him credit for; he even disarmed me! All right, he's quite a bit smaller now but I'd recognise Scar anywhere! His reduced size must be a side-effect of resisting my oblivoration spell.'

Silas slumped down into one of the few remaining chairs and just stared at Becky.

'Wait, he thinks *I'm* Scar? This could be just the break I need.'

Becky stared impassively back at Silas, now was not the time to lose her cool. With one hand still tightly gripping the protection potion, she had safely completed the first and most dangerous stage. She had made contact with Silas … admittedly she now had to pretend to be her brother, Scar, but that would be an easy deception to pull off, especially as Silas already appeared to be convinced of it. Becky then began to feel the effects of her long and arduous journey and she yawned.

'Now what? Is he preparing to strike back … get even for what I did to him.' Clumsily, Silas picked up his wand from the floor but it still shook too much in his hand to be of any use to him. 'Maybe he's just tired … that's it, he needs to rest … this might be my chance.'

Silas nervously stowed his wand and retreated to the bedroom. Moments later, he reappeared carrying an old hatbox, one of his scarves and a small dish. Then he busied himself at the kitchen table. All the time Becky kept her eyes firmly fixed on him and Silas was well aware of the fact.

'Th-there you go, old friend ... no hard feelings, just a misunderstanding, eh?'

Becky yowled and Silas dropped the tin dish, scattering chunks of kibble over the floor. Quickly, Silas gathered the contents together again and added some more from a large cardboard box.

'What's this ... *Fishy Kibble*, hmm,' Becky read from the carton, '*everything a cat needs*. That's a stroke of luck.'

However, she did not eat just yet. First, she watched as Silas backed away again to the safety of his bed where he climbed back in and tried to settle down. It was to be a fitful and agitated sleep as his conscience reminded him of his past behaviour to Scar.

Becky tried the kibble and actually found it quite tasty. Then she rubbed the protection potion all over the hatbox before finally climbing in to sleep.

'Right, so far so good but let's see what the morning brings before we relax too much ... you're doing it again, Becks, talking to yourself. Well I doubt I'm going to get much sense out of *him* so I might be doing this for a while!' Becky then closed her eyes to sleep.

CHAPTER FOURTEEN
From Small Beginnings

As morning broke, it found Silas sitting up in bed and wide-awake, having hardly slept a wink all night. Becky on the other hand had slept like a log. She peered over the rim of her hatbox at Silas and yawned. Silas winced.

'Now what Becks? Well, you're still talking to yourself for one thing! He's clearly expecting trouble so, maybe a peace offering, to get him in a good mood *and* throw him off balance. I need to keep him guessing.'

Becky considered what would make a suitable offering for a crotchety old wizard teetering on the brink of dark magic. She thought back to the very first wizard, Ezra, and to the colony's first encounter with the Grimdyke wizard line. The story was told of the first cat to go with the Grimdykes as his familiar. She was called Bess and she had made a gift of a small mouse to the wizard. The legend told amongst the colony, explained that Ezra approved of his gift so much, that he stowed it away in his pocket. Becky wondered if such a gift might reach out to Silas and touch a part of him that she hoped still lay buried somewhere deep inside.

'Right, a mouse it is then but he'd better take good care of it!'

Becky dashed out of the croft and Silas heaved a great sigh of relief. Then, suspecting he had probably not seen the last of his revitalised familiar, he set about cleaning up the croft and throwing out the remains of the shattered furniture and gone off food. When Becky returned, some minutes later, she hardly recognised the place. Fear, it seemed had been a great motivator but that was not really the way Becky wanted to do things. As soon as Silas saw Becky, he returned to his bed and this time, Becky followed. She sprang effortlessly onto the mattress to sit next to him where she deposited her nervous cargo at Silas' side.

Silas looked down at the petrified mouse and a terrible thought occurred to him.

'Oh, no! He expects me to eat it! What else could it mean?'

Wary of the great power his cat appeared to wield, Silas picked up the creature by its tail and looked at it.

'Well, I suppose it's either this or oblivoration,' Silas thought.

Then he raised the mouse to his mouth where it hovered for a moment while Silas plucked up the courage to eat it.

Realising that Silas had misunderstood but not wishing to give the game away, Becky hissed at Silas and put a paw on his other hand. Silas froze and so too did the upturned mouse.

'What am I to do with it?' Silas asked Becky.

Becky thought for a moment then she dashed to the large potions cupboard hanging on the wall. Neither mouse nor wizard dare move but both followed Becky closely with their eyes. After a few minutes of frantic searching, all the time watched by a stunned Silas and upside-down, nervous mouse, Becky returned with another of her potions. After rubbing the ingredients together in her paws, she gestured to Silas that he should lower the mouse so that she could reach it. By now the mouse was a little light headed from being held the wrong way up and well past the point of being scared. Then, as Silas continued to hold the creature's tail, Becky carefully blew the potion over it. Straight away, the cloud of ingredients made the mouse cough and squeak, after which it wriggled a bit before falling still again. As the dust settled, Silas could now see that he was holding the tail of a pure white mouse and he then to his great relief he realised that it was meant to be a pet and not some form of terrible ingested revenge.

'What? This is a gift, after what I did to you?'

Silas was completely wrong footed and laid the shocked mouse down on the bed next to Becky after which he walked into the kitchen where he began sorting through the boxes and tins on a high shelf.

'Well,' Becky said to the mouse. 'You said you wanted an easier life than you had on the moors!'

'Yes I know but I wasn't expecting this ... not with him! I though he was going to eat me.'

'So did I ... just for a moment. He must really be worried about what I might do. Well it's not a bad way for him to start. He bullied Scar so I suppose it's only natural that he would expect to be bullied in return so we'll see how he behaves.'

Silas saw Becky talking quite openly to the mouse and it only strengthened his belief that his familiar possessed some pretty special powers, powers that *he* had only been able to dream of. Silas returned to the bedroom.

'Will this be suitable?'

Silas set a large mesh cage on the bed. It was something his father had used from time to time but he had never taken much notice of what he used it for. Now however, it seemed ideally suited to the needs of his new houseguest.

'What do you think?' Becky asked the mouse.

'Well it's alright, but I don't want to be locked in. I want the cage door leaving open. I'll also need some food and something to drink, oh and some bedding would be nice.'

'Of course, I think that can all be arranged.'

Becky left Silas and the mouse together and ran to the kitchen. Silas eyed the mouse warily and the mouse stared defiantly back. Seconds later, Becky returned with a mouthful of her own kibble and Silas took the hint. He then provided a small dish of water and the top off a jam jar to hold the kibble. Once again, Becky visited the potions cupboard, this time returning with a paw-full of twigs. Using the twigs, she stirred the mouse's water and it turned orange. The mouse sniffed and appeared to approve of the improvement and of his new arrangement.

'I can't keep calling you "mouse". What is your given?' Becky enquired.

'My kin called me Septimouse, because they said I was the seventh in the litter.'

'Well Septimouse, welcome to your new home. If there is anything more Silas or I can do for you, just let me know but don't forget your part of the bargain. You will be my eyes and ears when I am away from the croft.'

'It's a deal!' the mouse agreed.

Once again, Silas watched as Becky talked with his new houseguest but he could only wonder about what had passed between them. With Septimouse comfortably installed on the dresser next to the potions cupboard, Becky turned to Silas and waited for her first instructions as his un-familiar cat.

'Ah ... right then ... er ...' Silas fidgeted nervously under the gaze of the apparently indestructible cat.

At this point, Becky could have quite easily told Silas what to do but talking to humans was a card she played with caution. Where Silas was concerned, it was worth keeping that particular card close to her chest, at least for now. Realising that Silas was still a little shocked and less than rational, Becky thought that he could be better employed cleaning up the croft. To give him a clue to what he should do, she first used a new potion to reverse the aqua-fermentum spell that Silas had used on the water. Then she dragged a small discarded milk carton to the bin, where she first looked sternly at Silas then at the carton, before dropping it in.

'Right! More cleaning it is then,' Silas nervously replied.

As Silas began his chores, Becky headed for the cat flap but not before she had signalled to Septimouse that he should keep his eyes on Silas while she was out. Then, just so that Silas behaved himself and without turning to see his reaction, Becky expertly evaporated an empty matchbox lying by the kitchen door.

'Perrr-futt!'

The box vanished in a small puff of smoke and as Becky left, she could hear the sound of sweeping quicken.

'Right, that should keep him busy for a while. Let's take a look at this moor. Daylight is always the best time to investigate but just in case …'

Becky made a mental note to gather the ingredients needed to create a stunning potion, should one be required. Scar's old collecting bag was the perfect accessory and soon she had enough potion mixed to subdue a bull, if necessary. From the top of a large boulder, Becky tried to get the lay of the land. The pathway she had taken from the mine level led from the croft, along the foot of Highfell Ridge and following a small stream, until it disappeared out of sight at the far end of the valley. Looking in the other direction along the trackway, Becky could see that it led across the moor to the village of Skellside. That would be a journey for another day; today she would investigate the stream and the likelihood of food. For the moment, Silas was most attentive but if he forgot or slipped back into his old ways, Becky knew that she would need another source of nourishment.

Trotting along the grass track that led to the mine, Becky felt pleased with what she had achieved so far but she was far from being complacent. She knew that if Silas was to be turned back to good magic, it was likely to be a long and slow process and he needed to make the choice freely. The trackway made for easy and fast travel but from her position between parallel rows of high drystone walls, she could see little of her

166

surroundings. She remedied this by jumping up onto the wall and picking her way along the top. From her new elevated position, she could now see across the moor to her left and to the right, to the bridge that led across the stream. The water that drained out of the mine joined the beck at this point and Becky studied the effect that the mine water had on the stream. Upstream of this point the water was rich and filled with life. Reeds, fish, voles, in fact all manner of creatures used the water for hunting and travel but below it was a different story. A few sickly looking weeds and the occasional pale fish were all that Becky could see.

'Right, upstream good, downstream bad,' Becky repeated to herself.

'I hope you're not thinking of diving in there!' a familiar voice cautioned from beside her. 'You should stay upstream or you'll end up as barmy as Dingle.'

It was Norman and he was proudly sporting a new tail.

'Grew back overnight it did. The tingling kept me up for most of the time but it was worth it.'

'Glad you approve,' Becky replied.

'There's just one thing.'

'Yes ...' Becky replied fearing Norman was up to something.

'I *sort of* told a few friends and well ... life here is hard and some of them aren't doing so good ...'

'And you said I would help them.'

'I suppose it *might* have sounded like that.'

'Ok, so how many are there?'

'Only two, for now. This is Radar and Grabbit.' Two slightly sceptical rats then appeared at Norman's side.

'Are you *absolutely* sure Fur-splash is safe, that's one big cat if you're wrong!' Radar enquired timidly.

'Look at her paws. There are more blades there than on a Swiss army knife!'

'A what?' Becky asked blankly.

'I told you ... she doesn't get in much ... she's a Greyfell!' Norman explained to his friend.

'So she really is a milliar then?' Radar asked.

'Not exactly,' Becky replied, 'but I'm hoping to be one day. I'm standing in for my brother who retired ... er, through ill health,' she added tactfully.

'Blasted him, Silas did!' Radar explained. 'Terrible temper that one.'

'Oh, you know then.'

'Not much escapes a rat, especially a rat like Radar but that brings me to why he's here,' Norman explained slightly sheepishly.

'You mean you want me to do something about his missing e-a-r?' Becky replied.

'Eh?'

'What is it with rats! His *ear*!'

'Oh, right. Why didn't you say so in the first place?'

'I guess my exploration of the moor will have to wait until another day. Come on, follow me and I'll see what can be done. While we're on the subject, what's wrong with Grabbit?'

'Dropsy! Well, that's what we call it. He seems to have caught a "clumsy bug" from somewhere ... in fact it was the last thing he caught first time!' Norman laughed.

If Silas could have seen the sight that followed, he would probably have packed his things and left the fell for good. As Becky trotted back to the croft, followed by her three new companions, she looked like the pied piper of Hamlin. Arriving back at the croft Becky suddenly realised that she had a problem. She could not very well take Radar, Grabbit and Norman inside as Silas might become suspicious. She needed an outdoor surgery, somewhere close to the back door and easy access to the potions cupboard inside but all out of sight of Silas. In the yard at the back of the croft, stood an upturned cast iron bathtub, well, at least half of one, it appeared to have fallen casualty to Silas' bad temper and equally bad spell casting. This was perfect for Becky's needs and while the rats hid under the tub, she returned to the potions cupboard to gather ingredients.

Seeing his familiar return, Silas snapped awkwardly to attention and awaited Becky's comments on his work. Becky was actually quietly impressed and Silas now had the croft looking clean and tidy. She ignored Silas, prolonging his agony a little longer and climbed up to the cage where she spoke to Septimouse.

'How have things been while I've been out?'

'He's never stopped! Washing, scrubbing, tidying, he's even changed your water and refilled the kibble dish. I think he's still in shock.'

'Good, he needed shaking up.'

Becky opened the store cupboard and removed an assortment of ingredients. Then she returned to the cat flap, all the time watched by Silas. As she left, Silas heaved a great sigh of relief. Septimouse then squeaked loudly, which spurred Silas into another fit of polishing and dusting. Outside, Becky attended to the two rats, watched over keenly by Norman. Despite their nerves, both Grabbit and Radar, stayed in the consulting tub with Becky where she began their treatment. First, she crushed together the ingredients, which she would apply as a poultice to the site of the missing or damaged part. Then, she applied one potion to Radar's ear and the second she plastered all over Grabbit's paws. Minutes later, Radar and Grabbit were sat side by side, waiting as the potion took effect.

Radar's head occasionally shook as if he were being bothered by a fly, while the green mush perched on top of it did its work. Grabbit sat with both his paws in what looked like a green muff. He shuffled and fidgeted nervously as first Norman then Becky inspected their progress.

Suddenly, the drying dollop of green on Radar's head was flicked off by his newly re-grown ear.

'*One down one to go!*' Becky whispered to Norman.

'I heard that!' Radar replied excitedly as he proudly washed his new ear.

After that, the green poultice around Grabbit's paws began to tighten as it too started to dry out. Then the wrap broke and fell in two. Grabbit instinctively caught the two halves as they fell towards the ground, intercepting them before they hit.

'Did you see that? I'm cured! The Grabster is back! How can I ever thank you Fur-splash ... I mean. Becky?'

'Well, to begin with, you could remember to call me Whitescar, at least around Silas ...'

'Ahem!' Norman tried to interrupt Becky but failed.

'The last thing I need is for him to realise who I am ...'

'AHEM!'

'Secondly ...'

'A-H-E-M!'

'What is it Norman? What I have to say is important.'

'Silas doesn't speak rattish, felish or avian, in fact he barely speaks human!'

'Oh right, sorry Norman, good point. In that case Grabbit, Radar, you are quite welcome. Just take care of your ears and paws in future. From what I've heard, you'll need them out there on Barren Moor.'

The three rats thanked Becky repeatedly before finally leaving for home. Becky felt good for what she had done but now wished she could have the same success with Silas. Becky knew that she needed to stop him reverting to his old ways but how to go about it, that was the problem. As she returned to the croft, Silas once again snapped to attention. Becky had an idea and climbing onto the freshly scrubbed kitchen table, she found what she was looking for. She carefully pushed a teacup towards Silas then stepped back and looked slowly from one to the other.

'Oh, you want me to fill it, but I didn't think cats drank tea.'

Becky tilted her head to one side and stared at Silas.

'Ok you're the boss.'

Becky watched as Silas boiled the water and then filled the cup. Then he went to the kitchen cupboard for the tea bags and milk. Silas returned to the table looking a little worried.

'I'm sorry there are no teabags left, I forgot to get them.'

Becky looked at Silas. He was grubby, tired and still trembling. She jumped down from the table and scaled the chair by the potions cupboard watched closely by the mouse.

'Are you sure you know what you're doing?' Septimouse enquired.

'I think it's time to take this relationship up a notch,' Becky enigmatically replied.

Returning to the kitchen table where Silas still sat nervously with milk carton in hand, she walked over to the cup of hot water and dropped in some of the retrieved leaves. Silas stared at the steaming brew and without him needing to say a single word Becky could tell what he was thinking. In fact, Silas was in no doubt, he thought his time had come and all that was left to him now was to take the honourable way out. Becky has seen enough.

'It's herbal tea!' she finally said to Silas, 'and it's for you.'

Silas immediately dropped the milk carton, spilling it all over the tabletop. Then, immediately realising what he had done, he quickly stood up the carton again.

'You ... can ... talk! At least, I can understand what you're saying ... how is that possible?'

'Drink your tea, it's been a long day ... for both of us,' Becky replied softly and then she lapped up some of the spilt milk as Silas tried to drink his tea.

The cup in Silas' hand trembled splashing tea down his shirt. Becky shook her head slowly and left the table for the comfort of her hatbox bed and a well-earned rest, but before she closed her eyes to sleep, she peered over the lip of the box to look at the shell-shocked wizard.

'Good night Silas,' Becky said softly.

Silas opened his mouth to speak, but no words came out.

CHAPTER FIFTEEN
Flawed Fauna

Over the coming months, as the popularity of her outdoor surgery continued to grow, Becky began treating an increasing number of creatures from Barren Moor. Silas slowly overcame his habit of jumping to attention every time Becky entered the room but he was not yet completely at ease with her. This was partly due to what he saw as her sixth sense. He still had not been able to join all the dots and remained unable to see that Septimouse, true to his word, kept watch over him in Becky's absence, reporting to her everything that Silas had or had not done. Eventually, they began to settle into a reasonably agreeable routine. Most days, Becky would awake to find at least three or four small animals sheltering under the bathtub in the backyard and it was not long before she was treating all manner of ailments and infirmities.

Silas of course, remained completely unaware of the activity in his back garden, excusing Becky's strange behaviour as being "peculiarly cat-like and none of his business". If ever he got too curious and tried to look out of the kitchen window, Septimouse would squeal loudly, alerting Becky and shocking Silas back to work. The role of master and servant, it appeared, had come full circle and where Silas had once ruled with an iron fist, now Becky held sway. The time was approaching when Becky would need to set things right and Silas, face his destiny and become the wizard Ethan hoped he would but they were not quite there yet.

Becky continued to explore the dower moors, gathering plants and seeds, and mapping the many runs and hunting grounds as she grew more familiar with them. Even Barren Moor it appeared improved on closer inspection. Although it had no protection charm, many creatures that hunted there came to an unofficial understanding with Becky. They soon realised that it was in their best interest not to interfere with the stranger as she went about her odd business. Besides, they never knew when they might need her services to heal a wound, ward off a fever or remove the poison from a bite or sting.

Becky fed in the stream where it was safe, and when Silas had the money to buy it, she ate the fishy kibble he supplied. The turning point in their relationship really came when the moor began to echo with tales of a most bizarre rescue. Creatures began hearing, from reliable sources, that the new milliar had actually treated one of the flying-death. Soon the legend began to spread of how the Highfell milliar found a fledgling osprey and instead of evaporating it, she began talking to it. The story told how this flying killer had broken its great hooked beak in an accident and was now unable to hunt or feed. All that stood before it was a slow and painful death as it starved. The part of the rumour that puzzled the creatures most was when they heard that the milliar, caught fish to feed to the bird, while its beak grew back and as a result, the bird now keeps watch over the milliar when it is out on the moors. Even more bizarrely, if that was possible, it was rumoured to be only one of many flying creatures, the milliar had helped.

Unaware of her growing reputation, Becky continued to encourage Silas, while treating the growing number of visitors in her bathtub-surgery.

'I thought I might try reading my father's old potion book again,' Silas announced quite unexpectedly one quiet evening. 'It's always been double Dutch to me before but now I've seen what *you* can do with potions … well, I thought I'd give it a try.'

'It is in your blood, Silas, as it was with your father. What you lack is the confidence,' Becky replied. 'Try something simple to begin with.'

Silas went to the potions cupboard and removed a small hand-written notebook. Then he sat across the table from Becky and she watched with interest as he read.

'How about a spell to clean the house?' Silas asked cautiously.

'How about a potion to purify water, making it safe to drink?' Becky suggested. 'Magic is for the benefit of others, not to support greed or laziness. Selfish spells have hidden consequences, ones that can't be avoided.'

Silas nodded his understanding.

'Right, so no personal gain. Got it.'

At last, Becky's patience with the wizard was beginning to show results and accepting her advice, Silas flicked through the faded pages until he found another potion to try.

'Here's a potion to make sweet water,' Silas said.

'Good, start there.'

Silas walked to the cupboard and reading from the book as best he could, he tried to interpret the symbols on the bottles and boxes. Some minutes later, he returned with a selection of jars and a small mixing bowl.

Setting them on the kitchen table Silas then began adding ingredients to the bowl, watched closely by Becky. One by one, Silas read off the ingredients and added them to the mix but when he reached the final ingredient, Becky suddenly hissed at him.

'Sorry, but you were about to add monkshood! That could only have led to the forever-sleep.' Becky then carefully replaced the jar in the cupboard, returning with the correct ingredient. 'You must always double check, sight and smell, before adding.' Becky then dropped in the last ingredient and the brew fizzed and sparked. 'See, that's how it should react.'

Silas did see. He saw that he had just been saved from a terrible fate. If he had drunk water infused with the potion, it would have meant his certain end.

'I've been a terrible, terrible wizard ... not even that, I've been a terrible *failed* wizard! You could have had your revenge on me a dozen times over by now but still you try to help me. I just don't understand.'

Becky took some of the brew to a large pitcher of bog-grog; one of the last Silas had yet to throw out. Adding the potion made the liquor fizz and boil. When the activity had subsided, Silas looked at the crystal-clear water that had replaced the foul brew.

'There can be goodness in even the most unlikely vessels. Drink some; we need to have a long talk,' Becky suggested.

She could see that now would be the right time for some straight talking.

'I am not the familiar you once knew. The one you banished was my brother, Whitescar.'

A look of genuine remorse suddenly spread across Silas' face.

'He's not ... *dead*, is he? Tell me I didn't sink so low that I killed my own familiar.'

'Scar is alive ...'

Silas sighed and pleaded to know more about the fate of his old companion. Becky explained what had happened and how she came to take his place. She also told Silas how three ex-familiars had given her the knowledge she needed to replace Scar and why, when it would have been so easy, she had not taken her revenge on him.

'Can you forgive a misguided and resentful fool?'

'In time ... you still have much to learn and a difficult journey ahead of you but I will stay as your companion until my time is up and I must return to Greyfell. Now I think you should try another potion.'

Silas smiled and for the first time since he was handed the keys to Highfell Croft, he could see more than just gloom and disappointment in his future. Silas studied hard under the guidance of his new familiar and with the passage of time, he began to understand the real power of magic and the inheritance left to him by his father.

As months turned to years and curiosity began to get the better of the villagers, one by one, they ventured across the moor to see the new familiar and the reformed wizard. Becky's treatment of wild creatures soon expanded to include some of the pets of the village as word reached them of her skills. At first, the animals would leave their homes to visit Becky on their own but soon they were being accompanied by their owners to be treated by Silas himself. At last, Silas was able to experience the wizarding reward he so desperately sought. It had not been in the bog-grog, the power to banish or evaporate objects but in the appreciation and friendship that resulted from helping others.

As his confidence grew, Silas moved on to treating and advising villagers, while Becky continued to treat animals in the backyard surgery. Silas was now proficient at soothing sunburn, withering bunions and corns, easing strained muscles and loosening frozen limbs. In addition, he looked years younger, now that the lines of bitterness and resentment had faded from his face. Silas was a new man and well aware of how close he came to being lost forever. He was also aware of the great part his new un-familiar played in his recovery.

'Well my friend, today was a good day. I healed a nasty cut on Mrs Arkwright's arm, drew poison from a snakebite, and set a broken finger for Kershaw's boy. I know you've been busy all day too so I have a treat for us tonight. The villagers brought me some leftover cold-cuts and I have caught some fish for your supper.'

Becky climbed the chair next to the kitchen table and peered over the top.

'Here, try this; it will lift you up a little.'

Silas set a small box on the chair that brought Becky up to table height. Then, after a few minutes of activity at the old range, he brought two plates to the table, one for him, the other for Becky. Silas tucked in to his supper while Becky simply stared at hers.

'I took all the bones out of the fish and poached it in a little milk with some herbs,' Silas explained but then it dawned on him. He reached across the table, took a spoonful of the fish and ate it. 'I hope one day I will have earned your trust.'

'One day,' Becky repeated, and then she ate her supper.

After the meal, as the two sat and reflected on the day, Silas in the last of the armchairs and Becky in her hatbox, they heard a dull thud on one of the windows. A small bird out late on the moor had collided with it. Confused by the light inside, it had thought the window was open.

Becky immediately dashed out of the croft through the cat flap and round to the fallen bird. Minutes later, she returned with the limp body of a young goldfinch in her mouth. She placed it on the stone floor at Silas' feet and looked up to him.

'Is it dead?' Silas asked.

'Not yet.'

'How is it that you are able to fight your most basic instincts like that? I have never met a cat like you before, never met one that could turn down such an easy snack.'

'When you understand your food better, sometimes it makes it difficult to eat.'

Silas was beginning to understand what made this particular cat so special. He bent down and picked up the small finch but it remained limp and lifeless in his hands.

'This creature is beyond even your potions my friend.'

'I know,' Becky replied. 'That is why I brought it to you.'

'But I can't spell-cast! I never could.'

'Not true, you can't because you have never really wanted to … never *needed* to for the sake of another.'

'I don't understand.' Silas sat back in the chair clasping the bird carefully between his hands.

'The greatest of all deeds are those that go unrewarded, the greatest spells ever cast are those that are cast selflessly.'

As Becky talked and completely unnoticed by Silas, a slight glow shone from his hands to envelope the bird as he held it. Suddenly it fluttered into life and began to struggle.

'Talk to it, tell it not to panic. Tell it I won't hurt it,' Silas pleaded with Becky.

'This is your patient and your moment,' Becky replied and together with Septimouse, she watched to see what Silas would do next.

Silas raised up the captive bird to speak to it but he did not possess Becky's gift of language. He tried to tell the bird not to worry and that it was healed, although he still did not quite understand how it had happened. The bird continued to struggle and fearing it might hurt itself again, Silas opened a window and set it free. As the startled goldfinch flew away over the moors, Silas looked back at his hands.

'It pooped on me! Look!'

'Sometimes that is all the reward you get!' Becky replied, sagely. 'Besides it's supposed to be good luck.'

Silas looked back at his hand again and at his parting gift from the small bird. Then he started to laugh. 'I hope a wizard's wages aren't always this low!' Silas then washed, after which he returned to his armchair and still with a broad grin on his face he confirmed, 'As I said before, this has been a *very* good day.'

'I quite agree,' Becky replied and for the first time in all their months together, she climbed onto the armchair and sat down beside Silas where the two remained until it was time to sleep. Silas laid his hand on Becky's neck and gently stroked it.

When morning broke Silas looked out onto the moor. Somehow, it looked different this morning, not as dull or as forbidding as it usually appeared.

'Time to do some exploring, I think and time to shake off these old cobwebs.'

After washing and dressing, and for the first time in many years, Silas stepped onto the moors to wander the tracks and cart-ways. Everything about it looked unfamiliar, as if he were seeing it properly for the first time. The last time he had walked there, he had been just a boy. It was back in a time when the locals used to visit the croft regularly to seek the advice of his father. Silas thought back to the incredible things he had seen him do. With a practised flourish of his wand, Ethan had inflated punctured car tyres and revived sickly dogs when they were born too soon. He had rid entire flocks of sheep of a fatal illness and cured a sheepdog of poor eyesight but at the time, Silas had shown little real interest in his father's work. Even when Ethan had created a special magical bottomless bag of sweets for him on his birthday, he had taken it for granted and now he was alone with a lifetime of regrets and one last chance to set things right.

He had no idea how long he had wandered alone on the moor but as the sun set over the ridge, Silas vowed to make amends. He had the guidance of a skilful familiar and a renewed interest in good magic. He had even regained the support of the villagers, well, most of them. There were still a few amongst them with long memories and they found it hard to forgive but he was making progress. As it began to grow dark, Silas was firmly resolved to do better and he could not wait to tell Becky.

Back in the croft, as the light began to fade, Becky used flash powder to light the lamps around the room but she was beginning to grow concerned for Silas. He had now been gone for hours and it was not like him to stay out after dark. Leaving Septimouse in charge, she set out to enlist the help of a friend. A large barn owl called Specks, owed her a favour and it was time to call it in. Becky ran onto the edge of the moor and let out the strangest cry.

'*SCHREE!*'

This was a cry for help to her friend and not intended to be understood by anyone else. As her call echoed around the fell, Becky hoped nothing serious had befallen Silas. Despite his past actions towards Whitescar, she had now developed a soft spot for the reformed wizard. Unfortunately, Silas also had a soft spot but his was a particularly foul bog on the moor and in the dusk of evening, he had stumbled into it on his way home.

As silently as the night itself, Specks appeared and settled next to Becky on a short tree stump.

'You are getting better at our tongue but you still have the strangest accent,' the owl observed.

'Sorry, Specks, no time to chat. Silas hasn't returned tonight and I'm afraid he's still on Barren Moor.'

'That's a good place for an owl to be but not a wizard. Stay here, don't try to follow me yet, these moors can turn a person around. I'll be back when I have news.'

Specks flew off like a ghost in the dark. He would silently scour the moors from his vantage point on high, looking for any signs of Silas. Specks was Barren Moor's very own stealth spy-plane and Becky had all her hopes pinned on his powerful night vision.

Time ticked by and Becky grew more anxious. A young fox passed by as she waited. Luckily, it was someone she had helped on a previous occasion and it was not in the mood to fight. The fox immediately recognised Becky and stopped to see what was wrong.

'Becky? What are you doing out on the moor, alone, it's not safe you know.'

'Hi Minty, I've lost Silas.'

'That was careless. Where did you last have him?' the fox chuckled.

'This is serious!'

'And she's not alone!' Specks added from right behind the fox.

'Strewth, you need a bell round your neck. It's not good sneaking up on a chap like that.'

'Save it Minty, Specks doesn't speak vulpine,' Becky explained. 'Specks, please tell me you found him.'

The owl had found Silas lying on the ground where he remained motionless. Specks suggested that they both follow him onto the moor to where Silas was. Unprepared and potion-less, Becky gathered what she could along the way, hoping that whatever ailed Silas, she would then be prepared.

Becky and Minty found Silas by the side of a foul smelling dark bog. Minty tugged at Silas' jacket until he had pulled the wizard's head clear of the fumes coming up from the water. Becky then hastily blended a revitalising potion. After blowing the concoction into Silas' face, she waited for him to react. What seemed like an eternity passed by before Silas finally stirred.

'Is that you, Becky?' Silas croaked weakly.

'I brought some friends to help guide us but can you walk, are you strong enough?'

'That's twice you've saved me.' Silas got to his feet but he swayed from the effects of the marsh gas. 'Lead on, I'll be alright.'

With directions from Specks and the tracking skills of Minty, they lead Silas back to Highfell Croft, where he collapsed with exhaustion on the bed. Becky dragged the covers over him and thanked the others for their help. With their work done, Specks and Minty disappeared onto the moors leaving Becky preparing a stronger potion to help remove the last effects of the gas. Then she sat and waited.

CHAPTER SIXTEEN
Fever

When morning came, Silas appeared to have recovered a little. He looked much happier and was already up and organising breakfast for them both.

'I turned a corner last night ...' Silas began.

'Yes and nearly confoggated yourself to death in a bog!' Becky replied.

'I'll be fine. Your revitalising potion was most effective. As I was saying ... I am a new man,' but Becky could not help thinking that the old one looked a lot healthier. 'I am resolved to make up for my past bad ways by being all that I can and something my father would be proud of.' Silas then paused as a coughing fit robbed him of his breath, 'It's alright, just the last effects of the bog-gas wearing off.'

Becky tipped her head to one side and stared at Silas. Something was wrong, she had missed something but she was unsure what it could be. Silas *appeared* to be fine, just as he insisted but he looked a little pale and drawn.

'As soon as we have eaten we will open the doors to visitors and see what we can do to help them.' Silas had indeed turned a corner but at what cost to himself.

Breakfast was a fine spread and consisted of fresh, free-range eggs and home cured bacon from a nearby farm for Silas, fishy kibble for Becky and some herbal treats for Septimouse.

'Right then ...' Silas declared, 'time to see what can be done.'

What followed was an average sort of day, average that is for a wizard and a talking cat but by the evening, when the last visitor had been taken care of, Silas looked tired and drained. He was still cheerful, but he lacked the energy Becky was used to seeing in him. That night, Silas took to his bed early, saying that it had felt like a long day.

'I'm worried about him,' Becky admitted to Septimouse, 'he's not himself.'

'I think his colour has returned,' Septimouse replied encouragingly.

'Yes, but a little too much.'

During the night, Silas did something he had not done since Becky had joined him. He dreamed but whatever was ailing Silas it began to colour his dream. Tonight it appeared, was going to be a rough time, for all of them. Becky was already aware of Silas' ability to dream-cast spells from her brother but she had hoped to avoid experiencing it herself. At the same time, it was the very thing that had allowed her to hope that Silas would eventually be able to cast spells the normal way, with her help.

The night started peacefully enough but when Silas had been asleep for a little over two hours, Becky noticed a really bad smell in the room. When she looked out of her box, she could see that the large round hearthrug on the cottage floor appeared to have been replaced by a rank smelling bog. High up in his cage, Septimouse also watched as stagnant water began oozing outwards from the central pool, until it was covering most of the living room floor.

'What's happening?' Septimouse called down to her.

'Nightmares! When his mind is troubled, he casts spells in his sleep.'

'Will he be alright … wait, will *we* be alright?' Septimouse squeaked.

Then, as Becky's hatbox began to float on a sea of slime and ooze, she decided it was time to act and the safest place to be until it was all over, was the potions cupboard next to Septimouse. Taking care to avoid the seeping bog-water, Becky scaled the furniture to reach the cupboard and once there, she began mixing a potion that would reverse the dream-cast. As the level of bog water continued to rise alarmingly, Becky completed the potion.

'Arba-da-carba!' Becky called in felish and she threw the potion into the rising waters.

'I thought you couldn't spell-cast?' Septimouse pointed out.

'I can't. I can only do the odd *small* spell in felish. Most incantations don't translate and so they don't work for me … or worse still, they can backfire badly.'

This time it appeared Becky had it right and the foul-smelling bog evaporated in a hiss of steam, leaving them to wonder what Silas might conjure next. Throughout the night, images and manifestations from Silas' fevered mind, continued to appear. Sometimes chairs or tins of food would disappear only to be replaced by goblins, frogs or flashes of ignited marsh gas. At one point, a fully formed Jack-o-lantern strolled across the room, carrying his brightly lit lamp designed to mislead travellers. This remarkably real looking spectre walked across the floor to where Becky and Septimouse sat, only to pass straight through them *and* the wall behind, like a ghost.

'That was creepy!' Septimouse called from the corner of his cage. 'How long do you think this will go on for?'

'Till Silas' mind is at peace.'

'That long!'

'I *could* wake him and the dream-casts would be reversed but he really needs all the sleep he can get. We'll just have to stay on our toes.'

It was to be a long night for both of them as Silas' fevered imagination evoked all manner of strange creature, buried fear and insecurity. When at last morning came, it found Becky and Septimouse completely exhausted. Silas was the first to wake, claiming that a sound night's sleep had done him good but Becky could tell otherwise. Despite the brave face, Silas was still unwell and Becky remained at a loss to understand what was causing it. Before beginning work for the day, she created a new draught for Silas, designed to help him fight off the effects of the new fever. This stronger blend, coupled with a chest poultice, she hoped would set Silas right but in the meantime she would need to persuade him to rest and let her handle the visitors.

Although Silas appeared to rally with every new application of potion, by the end of each day, he would be as ill as ever. No matter what Becky tried, the best she could do was to delay Silas' symptoms. Each day he would feel a little better but he would then slip back into fever at night. Becky began to fear the worst. If she could not break the fever, she was afraid that they would lose the wizard, just when she had found the good inside him.

As the days slipped by, visitors to the croft began to learn of Silas' condition. They left flasks of hot soup, warm meals and drinks for him and waited for news. Silas had indeed reformed and once again, the whole village trusted the *new* Wizard Grimdyke as they had his father and all Grimdykes throughout the years. However, a dark cloud hung over the village as they too began to fear the worst and that Silas was not about to pull through. All through this dark time, children brought a steady supply of kibble for Becky and food pellets and other tasty cereals for Septimouse. The children had been sent by their anxious parents so that they could feed Becky and Septimouse, and then return with reports on the wizard's progress.

Soon, the villagers themselves began turning up for treatment, with little more than bruises or splinters in their fingers, just so that they could get the latest news on Silas. Just a glimpse of him might reassure them that he was well but lately, Silas spent most of his time in bed while Becky tended to visitors.

All the time, Becky continued to wrack her brains for a solution and she was not about to give up. She was a bright cat and could clearly remember all the potions her three tutors had passed on but none of them seemed to be enough to help Silas. Becky felt a great sadness that she was letting the wizard down but he remained cheerful, saying that everything happened for a reason and that she should not worry. A familiar should protect its wizard, Becky knew this but this had been an attack that she had not foreseen, neither was she prepared to deal with it. As evening fell and the visitors returned to the village, Becky checked on Silas before leaving again for the moor. She hoped to find some new ingredient or another familiar with greater experience but that was unlikely. Each wizard had his own area to watch over and the nearest was many miles away. Becky also knew that leaving Silas to find them would take too long and keep her away from him when he needed her the most.

Once outside, Becky ran towards the bridge that carried the cart track over the stream. There she sat and stared into the tea-brown waters below. She had been able to recall no new potions, no brew that would work any better than the ones she had already tried. The moor had already given up all the ingredients it could and no new ones existed. If Becky had thought that Whitescar's early return was bad news, her own early return with the news that Silas was dead, would be far worse and it would mark the end of the colony's long and harmonious association with the great wizarding line.

Just then, Minty passed by and stopped to enquire about Silas. Later, other creatures from the moor also found Becky and asked the same question but sadly Becky had only bad news for them and an admission, that she had done all she could. Having talked with most of her friends about the moor and other animals that had fallen foul of the bogs, a new theory was beginning to form in her mind. When they had found him, Silas had to be pulled clear of the water by Minty. Becky had always assumed that the terrible confoggation gas had been to blame for Silas' condition but what if he had also swallowed some of the foul water? This was a very worrying thought. Becky's mind spun as she thought about all the recipes she knew for anti-poisoning potions, water cleansing powders and invigorating draughts but all those that she could think of, she had already tried.

It was growing late and the moor was slowly coming alive with the calls of the many night creatures. Although she had not found the cure she hoped to find, it was time to return to the croft and see how Silas was fairing. No one that knew Silas could fail to be impressed with the way he had changed. They could see the improvement in both his nature and outlook but more than that, they could also see his father in his improved character. When Ethan had left Highfell Croft they all agreed that they had lost a good man, and now they feared they were about to lose another in his son.

Becky returned to the croft, a little afraid of what she might find. When she entered the kitchen, she could see that Septimouse was no longer in his cage. Instead, he now sat on the carved wooden bed head, watching Silas closely.

'How is he?' Becky enquired.

'Very still. His breathing is shallow and fast. Is he going to die?'

Even Septimouse, who had once though very badly of the wizard, was now afraid they were about to lose him.

'There must be something we can do; we've come too far to let it end this way,' Becky cried to Septimouse.

189

CHAPTER SEVENTEEN
Bless-you!

The only place left for Becky to look was in the old potions cupboard. Somewhere in the store of rare concoctions and ingredients, she hoped to find a cure, one she had previously overlooked. Fading labels on the various jars, declared their contents. Names like aconite that also carried many warnings, borage and calendula, dittany and feverfew; each had their role to play and when correctly combined, the resultant potion could be far greater than the sum of its individual ingredients. Mint, mandrake, purslane and valerian, were all equally powerful, in the right hands but none of them of much use to Becky right now.

'I don't know what to do!' Becky called to Septimouse.

'Stay there, I'm coming over.' Septimouse ran from the bed head across the floor and over to where Becky stood staring hopefully at the ingredients that lined the shelves. 'I can't believe I'm going to say this but, pick me up and set me on the shelves. I'll take a look for you. I can get right into some of the deeper shelves. Maybe you missed something there.'

Becky bent down and carefully picked up Septimouse in her mouth. She could not have been any gentler if she had been a mother with her first-born.

'That was … *unsettling*,' the mouse replied, 'but if I had to trust anyone …'

Septimouse was a most methodical mouse and decided that there was only one place to begin his search and that was

190

at the very top. This meant of course that he had a lot of climbing to do. Well aware of the passage of time, Septimouse set about his task at speed. He vaulted small pillboxes, scaled sharp metal graters and grinders, skidding around the inside of large mixing bowls before scrabbling up skeins of dried and twisted roots. Eventually he reached the topmost shelf.

'These jars have not been used for a very long time. From the scratch and sniff left on the labels, they are mostly poisons.'

'Be careful with those. The smallest part could send you into a forever-sleep,' Becky warned. Septimouse read out the ingredients but none of them appeared to be of any use. Then he spotted something lodged behind the jars.

'There's something at the back of the shelf ... wait I'll try to get a better look at it.'

Becky's small accomplice disappeared behind the rows of jars and bottles to emerged seconds later.

'I think it's another potion book. It's very old and really well hidden. I'll try to free it.'

Septimouse struggled to dislodge the notebook but he was only a mouse and the book was heavy. Becky heard the chink of jars being moved and stepped back from the cupboard.

'Are you sure you can do this?'

'Sure I'm sure, leave it to ... oops!'

As the book fell free from its hiding place in the cupboard, it was all Septimouse could do to stop himself from falling off the shelf with it. What he could not do was to stop the freed book from dislodging a number of potion jars from the shelves as it tumbled. What followed was an almighty crash of glass, tin and marble as bowls and bottles cascaded from the cupboard to smash on the hard, stone floor. Becky leapt backwards to avoid the avalanche but all she could do was watch helplessly as they shattered on the floor. They both turned to see Silas' reaction but he did not respond. He was sleeping too deeply to hear anything. A great cloud of dust and powdered potion ingredients billowed into the air like a starburst firework. Ingredients clashed with potions, elixirs combined with draughts and as they reacted and fought, the whole room twinkled and sparkled. Slowly the cloud began to settle.

'That's tor-tor-*TORN IT … ATISHOO*!' Becky spluttered. '*ATISHOO… A-TISHOO … A-A-TISHOO … TISHOO*!'

Dazed and now very dizzy, Becky finally stopped sneezing but when she looked up again, she could not believe her eyes. All the jars and bottles were back in their place.

'Septimouse, how did you do that so quickly?' she sniffed and rubbed the end of her nose.

'Don't look at me, I haven't moved. I've been hanging on to this dried dandelion root and trying not to fall.'

Then Becky noticed something else that was not quite right. Not only were the bottles back on the right shelf, in their rightful places but they were now completely unbroken.'

'But they smashed, I saw them break …'

'And I heard them!' Septimouse added. 'So what just happened?'

Becky thought hard but nothing she could come up with came close to explaining what had happened. Dismissing it for the moment, Becky turned to the reason for the crash. She walked unsteadily over to where the fallen book lay on the floor. Becky sighed when she discovered that it was not the potion book they had hoped for but an old personal diary belonging to Ezra. Becky was distraught. It had all been for nothing. Whatever the book contained it was not a much-needed cure for Silas' fever.

'Why couldn't it have been the *po-po-POTION BOOK*?' Becky sneezed loudly. When she opened her eyes again, lying on the floor in front of her was yet another book.

'What else do you keep up that nose of yours?' Septimouse asked in astonishment.

'I ... I didn't ... nothing? I don't understand.'

Becky looked a little closer at this new notebook. It looked to be as old as the diary but it smelled most peculiar. Becky read the writing on the cover.

"My little book of big spells, by Ezra Grimdyke.

All serious ailments dispatched and full health restored."

'What do you think it means?' Septimouse enquired, Becky just stared at the cover. 'We ... Silas that is, doesn't have much time.'

Becky opened the book and read again.

'It says that it's a book of spells, the most powerful spells Ezra knew.' Becky quickly flicked through the pages. 'It's *all* spells, there are no potions ... but I only do potions!'

'It wasn't a potion that conjured the book in the first place. It appeared because you needed it,' Septimouse pointed out.

'But I've wanted lots of things before and none of *those* have ever appeared.'

'Remember what you told Silas, "The greatest of all deeds are those that go unrewarded, the greatest spells are those cast selflessly". You needed the book to save Silas and at that moment you found the power to spell-cast.'

'But I didn't cast a spell,' Becky insisted. 'I just ... sneezed!'

'What were you thinking about at that very moment?'

'I was just thinking why couldn't it have been the spell book we found instead of the ... diary ... but I can't cast a retrieval spell, only a wizard can do that!'

'I think you may just be the exception,' Septimouse replied.

'What should I do, none of this helps Silas.'

As she spoke, the pages of the book suddenly fluttered open as if blown by the wind. As Septimouse stared in disbelief from his position, high on a shelf, Becky jumped backwards, startled by the sudden movement. Just then, the pages stopped and the book fell open at a drawing of a dark, dank bog. Underneath the drawing were the written words, "Salveo purgo-corpus".

'There's a paw-note written at the bottom of the page, it recommends a potion to use with the spell … it's the one I've been using on Silas.'

'It looks like you need to use the spell *and* the potion to completely cure someone of marsh-water poisoning.'

'I can't spell-cast …' Becky sighed.

'Do you remember something else you told Silas? You said he couldn't spell-cast because he had never really wanted to … he never *needed* to for the sake of another. You mastered potions and have never needed to spell-cast … until now. Even if you can't say the words, think them in felish … but more importantly, think about what you want to happen.'

'And then what?'

'Sneeze, I suppose … hey I'm only a mouse after all! I don't have all the answers.'

Becky read the words again picturing them in her mind and as she concentrated, she held the small book tightly in her paws and once again, she caught the peculiar scent of the old spell book. Then she sneezed!

'FISHOO!'

It could have been that he imagined it but Septimouse could have sworn that a cloud of firebugs sprang from Becky's nose when she sneezed. They flew to where Silas was lying and enveloped him like a shroud of twinkling mist, and as the tiny points of light settled, Silas began to stir.

'I feel *most* peculiar ... have I overslept?' Silas sat up in bed and looked around. 'You two look like you've seen a ghost. Is anyone else feeling hungry?'

Becky jumped onto the bed and for the first time, she purred. Silas was saved. The old spell of Ezra's had purged the fever from his body and restored him to full health, just as promised. Septimouse also made his way over to the bed to check on Silas but it took him a lot longer to get there.

Sitting on the bed in front of Silas were the strangest looking pair of friends he could ever have imagined but they were *his* friends and he would not have it any other way.

'A black cat that talks to other animals, a white mouse and a crotchety wizard, what a strange family we make but you know, somehow it feels *just* right.'

Becky and Septimouse stayed with Silas until he felt well enough to get up the next morning. The following day was quiet, bringing with it some much needed time off and time to recover. The Grimdyke Wizards had long ago set one day a week for themselves and nothing but the greatest of emergencies was allowed to disturb the peace. The croft was quiet and for once, bathed in sunlight. Silas drank another of the revitalising draughts prepared by Becky and apart from looking thin, he was almost back to his normal self. As Silas prepared to shave, he noticed the difference in himself in the mirror. His cheeks were sunken and his face lined beyond his years.

'I think I'll keep the beard. Somehow it looks ... right. So just how long *did* I oversleep by?'

Becky then explained the events of the past few days and what had really happened. She told Silas how it was now some seven days since his accident on the moor. Her potions had sustained him during his illness but it was a spell from Ezra's book that completed his treatment.

'Ezra, eh? He has a way of looking after people long after they have forgotten him. Well he won't be forgotten again and even if I *never* spell-cast, his book will still have pride of place in the potions cupboard.'

Septimouse then reminded Becky about the book that started the whole sneeze-casting incident and he wondered what had become of it. Septimouse had been so impressed with Becky's newfound skill that it was he that named her new power, "sneeze-casting". Becky picked up the diary and dropped it into Silas' lap. Silas declared that he had never seen the journal before. He had heard tales of his distant relative before but never felt connected with him somehow. Now he held his actual diary in his hands. Becky and Septimouse sat quietly with Silas as he read his great, great … Silas did not know exactly how many "greats" he was, but regardless, he decided that Ezra was a really "great" grandfather to have.

Having spent the rest of the day in a reflective mood reading about his great grandfather's exploits, Silas was finally able to draw a line under his own, old self. With Ezra's splendid character as a guide, Silas would continue to mend his ways and if he never became the great spell-casting wizard his father was, at least he had Becky and her magic sneeze to help him when things got difficult.

The following day, Highfell Croft opened for business as usual but neither Silas nor Becky were prepared for what was to come.

CHAPTER EIGHTEEN
The Missing Ingredient

Even before they had drawn back the curtains and before they had wiped the sleep from their eyes, they realised that something was different. There was a noise coming from the garden outside, a murmur they had never heard before. It was not the usual chatter of birdsong or the wind howling through the bushes, as it so often did on Barren Moor. It was the sound of people's voices.

Becky climbed out of her hatbox and stretched then she hurried to the back door to see what all the fuss was. Pushing her head through the cat-flap, she saw that the back garden was full of visitors.

'Is he getting up yet?' one small girl asked eagerly.

Becky returned to the kitchen to where Silas was getting washed and ready to face the day. Septimouse was performing a similar ritual in his cage on the dresser shelf.

'I think you had both better see this for yourselves.'

Silas walked over to the large cage next to the potions cupboard where he scooped up Septimouse in his hands and placed him carefully in his top pocket.

'Well, she did say we should *both* see whatever the commotion is,' Silas said to Septimouse as the mouse settled into the pocket.

With Septimouse poking out of his jacket top pocket so he could see and Becky by his side, Silas opened the back door. As it swung open, a great cheer went up. It appeared that everyone from the village was there. Somehow, news of Silas' recovery had reached the people of Skellside and they had all turned out to say how glad they were that he was on his feet again. Silas found it difficult to speak for a moment and he looked to Becky for some encouragement.

'Well, it's you they've all come to see, so say something!'

Silas smiled and with a small tear welling in his eyes, he addressed his new friends.

'I see you've all braved the banishing spell to get here,' Silas laughed softly. 'I really don't know what to say. I'm quite overwhelmed that you still care enough to come all this way to see me … after all I tried to do to you and the terrible way I behaved.'

'All in the past,' a small well-rounded woman called out from the front of the crowd.

'Doesn't he look like his father,' another whispered to the person next to them.

'Good to have you back, Silas,' a man called from the rear of the group.

'Mr Silas, sir, my hamster has hurt its leg.'

A small girl had pushed through the crowd and was holding up a small carrying cage for Silas to look at.

'Chloe, don't bother the man, it's his first day back at work,' the girl's mother chided.

'No, no that's alright,' Silas replied. 'It's business as usual. Come and see any of us any time you need to …'

'Except your day off eh, Silas!' another man chuckled from the crowd.

'Even then, if it's important,' Silas replied cheerily.

The crowd then began to disperse, apart that is from the small girl with the injured hamster but as the garden cleared, Silas could hardly believe what he saw. Every flat surface, chair or stone had on it a tin, bottle or jar of food. The villagers had all brought gifts to wish Silas well and a swift return to good health. No one had let on what they were planning to do although they all had the same thought and no one stayed behind afterwards to be thanked. They simply walked back to the village knowing that they could return to Highfell Croft anytime they needed help or if they just wanted to talk with the Wizard Silas ... or even Becky.

'Becky, would you like to see what can be done for this young lady and her small friend, while I gather up these wonderful gifts. If you go with my friend, here, she will see to your hamster's injury.'

The small girl went with Becky to the upturned bathtub in the backyard where Becky tended to the creature's leg.

'I don't see many of your kind here, are you new to the village?' Becky asked.

'Been here about four seasons,' the hamster replied. 'I fell off a bookcase the other day.'

'Yep, that will do it,' Becky replied as she rubbed a yellow ointment onto the injured leg. 'This will make it feel funny for a few seconds but it will pass.'

'Hey, it's getting *really* hot ... no, wait, now it's tingling ... now it's ... *ooh*, that's *really* strange. Now, it's stopped. Does that mean my leg is Ok now?'

'Try it.'

The hamster ran around the small carrying cage excitedly.

'Hey, no more pain! Thanks Clawpaw! By the way, my name is Norman and if you need any extra food for the small white one, just let my owner know, my treat ... well, hers really, she buys it.'

Becky smiled and then she thought for a moment.

'Norman?'

'Yes, why?'

'Do you ever see any of the moorland rats?'

'Not many but sometimes they come into my house for food. They tell me there's not much of it to be had on Barren Moor and what's there is hard to find. I did see one *really* odd

199

one once. He seemed to think he was a hamster! Rats eh, they get some daft ideas.'

'I think we have a common friend there,' Becky added.

'They are a bit, but good fun all the same,' Norman replied, missing the point entirely. 'My full name is Norman Auratus Higginbottom but I prefer Norman or just Norm.'

'Norm it is then, that way I won't confuse you with Norman the rat.'

'I should hope not!'

Just then, being unable to understand the noises passing between Becky and Norm the hamster, the young girl picked up the cage again, ready to go home.

'Oh, it looks like I'm going. Thanks Clawpaw. I mean, Becky,' Norman called. 'Tell the wizard it's nice to see him back on his feet too.'

Having cured her only patient of the day, Becky returned to the house but once inside their small kitchen all she could do was stare.

'This is all thanks to you, Becky. Without your help and guidance none of this would have been possible and I don't just mean the gifts.'

While she had been treating Norman, Silas had been busy ferrying the many gifts the villagers had brought, from the garden into their kitchen, where it now filled every available space. Becky studied the many shelves and cupboards filled with tinned meat, vegetables, fruit and juices and in one special cupboard, she found tins of fish, herbal treats and a large bag of cereal food for Septimouse. Some of the local children had also shredded a large bagful of colourful paper for Septimouse so that he would not run short of fresh bedding. To avoid any mix-up, they had even drawn a picture of him for the label.

'After what I tried to do to them I thought they would never speak to me again,' Silas sniffed, emotionally.

'It's rarely too late for change, and the villagers never gave up the hope that there was something of Ethan's goodness buried inside you, waiting to surface,' Septimouse explained.

'You know, for a mouse you can be worryingly bright sometimes,' Becky observed with her head tilted to one side.

'I guess we've all had our part to play in Ethan's plan,' Septimouse replied with a small grin and a twitch of his snow-white whiskers.

What followed was a quiet day and Silas suspected that the villagers were staying away to give him time to fully recover. Finding he had some time on his hands, Silas decided to spend it with Becky and Septimouse. He was now resigned to the fact that he would probably never spell-cast but he was determined to make up for this deficiency by becoming the best potions wizard he could be. It was equally unlikely that he would ever have the natural mastery of potions that Becky possessed but he was sincere in his efforts and as it turned out, a very good pupil. With help from Septimouse, Becky slowly explained to Silas the secrets of liquid magic and just as Nightfire, Raven and Luna had done with her, she passed on her skill to Silas.

The lessons progressed well over the coming days and Septimouse proved himself invaluable when it came to searching out the necessary ingredients. His natural scratch and sniff talents more than made up for his inability to read the labels and his un-natural understanding of magic frequently gave the others cause to wonder about their pocket-sized companion.

Brews, potions, concoctions and elixirs, Silas eagerly studied them all, and while he practised the art of potions brewing, Becky read from Ezra's spell books and in time, she too made steady progress. The turning point for Becky came when she finally accepted her own words of encouragement to

Silas and the very words that Septimouse had reminded her of in their darkest hour. Becky had always possessed the secret to spell-casting but the trigger was her desire to do good ... and of course, her magic sneeze.

As the year slipped by and summer turned to autumn, Silas, Septimouse and Becky were sitting by the window watching the Jack-o-lanterns dance and skip across the marsh. From the comfort and safety of home, they were fascinating, magical things to watch but close up, they could be a deadly distraction as both Silas and Becky knew all too well.

'I've been thinking ...' Silas began.

'Always a good way to start,' Septimouse replied sagely, if a little cheekily.

'It will soon be bonfire night and I thought a small display for the villagers might be in order ... just to say thanks,' Silas announced thoughtfully. 'With a combination of your spell-casting and my potions we should be able to put on quite a show.'

They all agreed. And in the days leading up to the great event, Silas, Becky and Septimouse would spend their spare time making enchanted fireworks and coloured flare potions. At night, they would read Ezra's diary and it was not long before they realised that the many small blanks left in his writing were actually hidden messages. Becky created a revelation spell to make the messages visible and together they learned more of the old wizard's more advanced magic. Until now, these special spells had remained hidden from all that followed, as had the book. However, with the right insight, co-operation and honest desire, they revealed themselves to be some very special magic indeed.

On his own, as Silas had once chosen to live, he was a miserable creature. He had been unhappy, bitter and resentful. He was also a failed wizard, and one whose future was decidedly bleak and tinged with dark magic. Now that was all in the past and with Becky as his familiar, Silas became all that he could be and worthy of the title Wizard Grimdyke. His father's wand along with his spell book, had pride of place in the potions cupboard and life at Highfell Croft settled into a comfortable and satisfying routine.

As the fifth of November drew closer, a messenger was sent to Skellside warning all pets and working creatures to stand by. The messenger was none other than Norman the rat who had a desire to meet with his namesake again and swap tails, his idea of a joke. Through the medium of Chinese whispers, all the pets and wildlife of the village began to pass the news round. The message was passed on from pet to pet, sheepdog to sheepdog, feral creature to feral, until all the animals knew the plan. At the sound of one lone thunderclap, they were to alert their owner's attention to the moors.

On the night, with everyone warned, including the natural residents of Barren Moor, Silas and Becky sent up the signal. It was a single spell of great power and resonance. With no flash or smoke to give anything away, it broke the silence with a loud grumbling bang. At that moment, every creature in the village turned to face the moors. Gerbils, rats, mice and hamsters, all ran to the end of their cage nearest to the moor. Dogs and cats pawed at doors or windows and birds perched on windowsills. Slowly the residents of Skellside also turned to face the moor.

Silas, Becky and Septimouse were ready. First, they sent up a cloud of crackling golden fireflies that flashed and twinkled in the night sky. This they followed with a barrage of multicoloured chrysanthemums of the most vivid hues, their massive fiery blooms filling the valley from end to end. As the large and showy flowers gradually subsided, another cloud of cracklers and hummers took to the sky, filling the fell with fizzing and chattering pops and whistles. Then came the special firework spells, the ones they were all especially pleased with and the most difficult to cast. The first to light up the moor was a forest of enormous green fern-like displays. Bright metallic green lights in the shape of towering tree ferns, danced across the moor as stars of red, blue and green exploded high in the sky to hover above the fiery foliage. As this awesome display faded, spiders and brightly illuminated orange pumpkin heads floated eerily across the open fell. Then, in the grand finale and against a backdrop of a cascading purple rain, huge firework mice skipped and ran, followed by a giant magical cat chasing a school of silvery fish and finally, the smiling face of Silas himself. As the fiery image of Silas winked to the village and then faded from view, loud clapping, cheers and whoops could be heard coming from the other side of the valley as the villagers showed their appreciation.

This magnificent display of magical cold-fire pyrotechnics had been an enormous success. The special smoke free firework spells had been enjoyed by all and Silas had been able to show his gratitude for all the gifts and concern they had showed when he had been ill.

The next day, many of the villagers visited the croft, few with any real problems or ailments but all expressed their thanks for the wonderful display.

CHAPTER NINETEEN
Scar's Return

A few days after the wonderful firework display, Silas was gazing out of the croft window and looking over the moor. He was thinking about the fiery images that had danced there, when another, even more unusual sight met his eyes.

'Becky, what do you make of this?'

Becky ran to the window and jumped up onto the sill. Becky was followed by Septimouse who was immediately curious, being naturally inquisitive by nature. Heading in their direction, down the small lane that led across the moor from Skellside, was a head. Whatever it may have been attached to was hidden by the tall drystone walls but the head appeared to know exactly where it was ... *headed*.

'That's a very tall sheep!' Septimouse declared. 'It must be nearly six feet tall!'

'It looks like a deer wearing a balaclava!' Silas added.

'Why would a head want to visit us?' Becky asked.

As the head grew nearer, the number of unanswered questions also grew, until it finally reached the front gate where they could all get a better look at the creature.

'Some idiot has stuck the head of a sheep onto a deer!' Septimouse clearly suspected that it was the work of a poorly trained wizard.

At that moment, a small man also came into view, standing at the creature's side and holding a leash. It appeared they were travelling together and had come expressly to visit

Silas but as she watched, Becky wondered where Silas would begin with such an odd-looking couple.

'Stay here while I go to see what they want,' Silas said and he left to greet the visitors at the front gate.

Becky and Septimouse watched as Silas talked with their new guests. Moments later, with presumably a better understanding of the situation, Silas lead the small rounded man into the garden and then round to the back yard, and the small man led the strange creature behind them. Becky and Septimouse dashed to the kitchen window where they could get better view of their new guests. The small man with the leash also appeared to be carrying a large bag, which immediately caught the attention of Septimouse. Its presence appeared to confirm his suspicions.

'I'll bet there's a head in that bag, the one that *should* have been attached to that deer! I reckon he wants Silas to do a head swap for him.'

'Its legs are too long for a deer,' Becky pointed out to the mouse.

'Maybe,' Septimouse considered, although not entirely convinced, 'whoever stuck the wrong head on could have stuck on the wrong legs at the same time.'

The small man was wearing a worn boiler suit and appeared to be quite concerned about his badly assembled sheep. Silas instructed the man to tie the creature's lead to a ring set into the wall of the croft next to the back door. The man did as he was bid and then he reached down to undo the holdall he had been carrying. Septimouse peered through the window to see what the correct head looked like.

'Now we'll see what sort of head it *should* have been!' Septimouse said excitedly.

However, instead of holding a spare head, the bag was full of fresh hay and as soon as the man had opened it, the creature began to feed. After another word with the man still attached to the other end of the leash, Silas opened the kitchen door.

'Becky, I think I might need your help with this one,' Silas said, poking his head though the opened back door. 'I think we're going to need your language skills to get to the bottom of this.'

While Becky stepped cautiously outside to investigate, Septimouse drew up a small tin on the windowsill to sit on, and an oat cracker to eat while he watched the scene unfolding outside.

'They tell me in the village that you're the chap to see about sick animals,' the small man explained to Silas.

'We have had some success,' Silas replied modestly. 'What's wrong with ... er, *it*?'

'Apart from having the wrong legs and someone else's head!' Septimouse sniggered from his ringside seat on the kitchen window ledge.

'He's been a bit down in the mouth lately, a bit miserable,' the small man explained. 'Not at all himself.'

'What do you expect, he's part someone else!' Septimouse chuckled.

Becky climbed onto the upturned bathtub for a better look at their strange long-necked visitor but she still was not high enough.

'I'm Becky. I help Silas with some of his visitors' problems.'

'Who sched that?' The animal had a very wet way of talking. It then looked down and saw Becky. 'Schorry I didn't schee you there.'

'Do you mind, you're spitting all over me!' Becky replied giving her fur a good shake.

'Schorry!' the animal sprayed again, looking quite genuine.

Becky stepped back a little until she was out of range, then she tried again.

'My name is Becky and I'm here to help you ... just as soon as I know what's wrong with you.'

'I'm Shceschill, I'm a llama, and we're schupposched to schpit!'

'Yes, but *all* the time?'

'I've got schumthing wrong with my moufh,' Cecil replied.

'*It looks like being more than just a shower*!' Becky muttered to herself. 'What *exactly* is wrong with it?'

'It's schlorr!'

'I had to ask!' Becky shook herself again. 'I'm guessing here a bit because I don't get to speak with many of your kind, but I assume you meant to say it is "*sore*", yes?'

'I sched *schlorr*, didn't I?' Cecil showered Becky again.

Becky looked up at the small man and Silas who by now were both struggling hard to stop themselves from laughing. In the kitchen window, all she could see of Septimouse were his feet and legs as he rolled around on his back, laughing uncontrollably.

'That's why I always wear these old overalls!' the man said to Silas. 'Oh, I'm Egbert by the way, no don't laugh, you'll only set off Cecil again.'

Becky looked back into the kitchen where Septimouse had climbed back onto his tin again but he was still holding his sides, laughing.

'I'd *like* to introduce you to Septimouse but I'm afraid you might drown him if you said *his* name,' Becky grinned. 'Do you think you could hold the shower for a minute while I look into your mouth ... no, don't say anything, just nod.'

Cecil nodded and after taking a deep, slurpy breath, he opened his mouth for Becky to examine.

'What's your cat doing, if Cecil goes off when she's that close, she'll never dry out!'

Then, as both Silas and Egbert winced, Becky put a paw into Cecil's open mouth. Seconds later, she removed a large thorn.

'Whoa! Thatsch better!' Cecil sprayed.

'I was afraid it might be,' Becky replied shaking herself yet again.

'Schorry,' Cecil said softly and only after turning his head this time.

'Don't go away. I'll give you something to take away the swelling,' Becky explained before jumping off the tub to head for the potions cupboard.

While she was preparing the potion, Silas and Egbert chatted in the yard.

'What made you keep llamas?' Silas asked.

'I didn't like sending the sheep to the … *you know where*, when they were older and so now I just keep the llamas for their wool, and don't laugh, for their company too. I live away on the hills and I hardly see a soul from week to week but these guys keep me company. I know it sounds barmy.'

'I think I understand,' Silas replied looking towards Becky. 'Even if they can't talk, animals can be good company.'

'I hope your friend here can help Cedric. It's not just me getting covered in … well, *you know what* … the real problem is the other llamas, they keep taking it the wrong way. They think he's being stroppy. He's got a really good temperament, our Cecil; it's just that he's like a lawn sprinkler when he's talking.'

In the meantime, Becky had returned with the ingredients for a potion in her collecting bag and once outside, she began preparing them. After pounding the ingredients on the upturned tub, Becky told Cecil to take another deep breath and then hold it while opening his mouth. Then she pressed the paste to the swollen gums and cheek.

'Thasch … humm, that's not too … ohhh, now ichsh getting hot! Now ichsh getting …'

'Could we do this without the running commentary, Cecil, I'm getting soaked here!'

Cecil sulked for a moment but then his expression began to change as the various sensations in his mouth kept changing, and again he was tempted to say something but decided better of it when he saw Becky's expression. After a few more minutes had passed and Cecil had changed his expression at least five times, he began to grin.

'That was brilliant! The soreness and swelling has completely gone. You're quite a familiar. Been doing this for long?'

'Not really and I'm not a real familiar, I'm just filling in for a friend,' Becky replied.

'He's a reformed llama,' Egbert exclaimed cheerily. 'I'd even got to the point where I was considering selling him to a punk revival band as a mascot, if I couldn't stop him spitting,' he chuckled. 'How can we ever thank you?'

'No charge, we're just glad to help.' Silas smiled, Becky was not quite as thrilled to have been in the firing line but then Silas added, 'It was really all thanks to Becky here.'

'Now if he spits, at least I'll know there is something wrong,' Egbert replied as he led Cecil away again.

'See you "*Shceschill*" and mind what you eat in future,' Becky called cheekily as Cecil walked away down the lane.

'Well,' Silas said straight faced, 'they didn't mention rain on the radio but you look like you got caught in a right downpour!' he chuckled. 'Come inside, I'll get you cleaned up. And as for that nonsense about you not being a *real* familiar, you're the best familiar any wizard could ask for, and then some.'

After Silas had rubbed Becky with a damp towel and cleaned her fur, she sat by the fire to dry off.

'We get plenty of variety in our line of work, eh Becky?' Silas thought aloud.

Becky was not as convinced as Silas that today had been *that* much fun but it was good to know that Silas now thought well of her. Septimouse on the other hand thought it had been a most entertaining day and kept mimicking poor Cecil's sprinkler talk every time he passed by Becky.

'Are you schettled in for the night now?' he would enquire, sniggering, 'or would you like some shclupper before you go to schleep?'

As they settled down to sleep after what had been a very unusual, if slightly damp day, they each wondered what tomorrow would bring. Life at Highfell was like that, unpredictable.

As a new morning arrived and dawn broke over the sleepy moor, Becky sat watching through the window towards the grey ridge. A blanket of mist still hung over the larger pools but the clumps of heather and banks of fern shone bright as the early sun began to warm the fell. Silas had finished washing and had just started getting breakfast for them, when Becky let out a yowl.

'What is it Becky?' Silas asked.

'Coming down the road … it's …'

'Not another walking carwash!' Septimouse laughed. Although how he knew about such things, they could only wonder. 'Two llamas in one week … it never rains but it pours, pours, get it?'

'No it's not a llama it's …'

Septimouse had had enough of the mystery and scrambled up to the window to see for himself.

'Oh no, it's another cat! I'm done for! Lock m-me in my cage, quick before it gets in here … what am I saying lock the door, don't let it in the croft!' Septimouse darted into his cage and shook under the pile of shredded bedding.

'Do you recognise who it is, Becky?' Silas asked, as he grew more curious. 'Let me see if it's one of our friends from the village.'

Then Silas peered through the window and his face dropped. Silas suddenly looked gravely ill, almost as ill as he had when he nearly died from the bog-water poisoning.

'What is it, a big hungry tom?' Septimouse asked timidly.

'Worse,' Becky replied, 'it's my brother, Whitescar.'

'Oh dear,' Silas said softly and he sank slowly into his old armchair.

'Let me see what he wants,' Becky replied.

'After what Silas tried to do to him, I could take a guess!' Septimouse said from beneath his quaking bedding.

Becky left the croft through the cat-flap and waited for Scar in the back yard. Apart from being unheard of that a cat should return to the croft after their time as familiar, Becky also wondered *why* he had come back. She waited patiently on the roof of her bathtub consulting room and eventually, Scar appeared at the far end of the yard. For a moment, he simply stood and stared at her. Becky looked at him, amazed that he had made it this far with little or no trail to follow and for once she was unable to gauge his mood. He always looked slightly menacing even when he was in a good mood simply because of his size. If anything Scar was even bigger now than when she last saw him but that was after spending time with Silas.

'You haven't been blown up then, sis?'

Scar finally spoke but still he gave little away.

'No, still pretty much in one piece.'

'How's he treating you?'

'Good, at least, he is now. He's not the same person you knew, Scar. He's changed.'

'There was certainly room for improvement.'

'It's good to see you Scar but …'

'Why did I come? I don't know really. Unfinished business, I guess.'

'With Silas?'

'With Silas *and* to see how you were coping and to make sure you were alright, also, I've got this problem with my coat. My fur just won't grow back evenly. I think I'm going bald from all the stress!'

Becky was eventually able to persuade Scar to sit under the upturned tub where she agreed to take a look at his fur-loss problem. His coat was certainly tatty and she suspected it was a condition caused by a combination of bad magic, poor potions and even worse diet. She also realised that Nightfire or Luna could have easily cleared up the problem for him without the need to make the long journey to the croft but Becky could also recognise an excuse when she saw one. She was very pleased to see her brother too.

'Wait here while I get something to fix that for you.'

While Becky returned to the house to prepare the potion, Scar withdrew to the far end of the yard again, where he could keep the croft in full view. Becky realised that it would be a simple job to re-grow Scar's missing fur and return his coat to full glossy health but she had another course of treatment in mind, one that she feared might take a little longer to complete. Moments later, Becky returned, potion in paw.

'This might … what are you doing over there?'

'Watching!'

'Watch later, for now, come back here where I can treat you.' Scar returned to the tub slowly and close to the ground. He did not intend to be caught off-guard by Silas for a second time. 'This may feel a little odd at first but given time, it *will* work.'

'Time? How much time?'

'Oh, it will take a few days to clear it up properly. You really should have seen me sooner.'

'Yes ... well, that was not really going to happen, was it?'

'Well now you've started you will need to continue with the treatment or ... well, you could go completely bald!' Becky thought a small white lie was called for at this stage. 'If you stay out here, there's a spring in the corner of the yard if you need water and I can bring you some food if you're hungry.'

'Not fish! I hope you've got something better than fish!'

'I've got something you might like and if you want somewhere dry and warm to stay ...'

'... I'm not coming inside!'

'No, I understand. I was going to say, you could use the old tea chest at the bottom of the yard. There's even an old blanket in there ... it's quite safe. Now don't forget, no running away or you'll go bald!'

Becky returned to the house and gathered some kibble for Scar. Silas had just bought a new large box but the old small box still had some in. Becky took it to Scar and once again made sure he stayed put. She could have cleared up his fur-loss problem as easily as sneeze but Becky had a more important problem she wanted to heal and that was the rift between Scar and Silas and that could take some time. Becky had one last warning to give Scar, and that was not to eat the small white mouse called Septimouse but Scar already knew about Ezra and the first white mouse. Despite his impatience, he had learned a surprising amount from his teacher, Luna, and would never have harmed a Grimdyke wizard's friend.

Having settled Scar into his temporary home, Becky returned to Silas. He was still looking grey and drawn because of the guilt he felt about the way he had treated Scar. Having turned away from the dark wizard he had become, Silas had been able to make amends for his past behaviour with all but Whitescar and he feared this would be his greatest challenge.

'How is he?'

'Well, but angry. He says he came here to see if I could help with his fur-loss but he really came to make sure I was all right and I think to see you again. I'm just not sure why.'

'Revenge? I deserve it … I even expect it.'

'I remember, but I think it goes deeper than revenge with Scar. I think what really hurt him was the disappointment. All his life he had heard tales of the great Wizards Grimdyke and he lived for magic and longed to be a part of it. From the moment he was chosen, all he wanted was to be a good familiar, the best familiar he could be and …'

'… All he got was me and I tried to … *kill* him. I let more than myself down when I turned away from good magic. As well as letting both you and Scar down I let the rest of the Greyfell Colony down as well. Then there are all the other Grimdyke wizards that came before me.'

'The villagers understand and they have forgiven you, and if you can prove yourself with one more good deed, then I will forgive you as well. I warn you though: this may prove to be your greatest test yet.'

Silas thought for a moment but he always knew what he would have to do one day. His greatest fear however, was that he would never have the opportunity.

'You mean … Scar, now? I thought he would prefer it if I left him alone.'

'He probably would but he needs to have his faith in magic restored, the way you restored my faith in the great wizarding line of Grimdyke. I don't think it will be easy but I know you have it in you … *now*.'

Silas forced himself out of his armchair. His arms pushed him from his hiding place and his legs carried him towards the window overlooking the yard but his mind still clung firmly to his sanctuary by the fireplace. Suddenly confronted by the view outside, it was as if he had just awoken. He saw Scar sitting in the tea chest lying on its side. Scar was so big it looked like he was wearing the chest as a jacket.

'He's ... still a very big cat, isn't he?' Silas said rather nervously.

Septimouse had found some courage from somewhere under the pile of bedding, and joined Silas at the window.

'Are you sure that's just one cat? He does know we mice are full of diseases ... doesn't he?'

'I thought that was rats?' Becky smiled.

'Well, it's worth a try,' Septimouse replied, retreating behind a box of candles.

'I gave you a protection charm a long time ago, remember, you're quite safe.'

'But you're not!' Silas pointed out to Becky. 'I haven't been able to spell-cast so you don't have full protection yet.'

'I'm not the one in danger here, not from Scar, besides, I have *some* protection at least as far as the rules of *self gain* will allow. I'm afraid this problem is beyond the power of magic to cure and I've already done all I can to help. The rest is up to you, Silas.'

Silas continued to watch Scar through the window for most of the day. Scar left his tea chest only to eat and drink but he never ventured close to the croft, unless Becky was there. Scar rarely took his eyes off Silas when he was at the window and this is how the first day was to play out.

The following morning, Becky replenished Scar's kibble supply and then applied a protection potion to the tea chest.

'Phew sis! What's that gunk?'

'Just a protection charm to keep you safe while I'm treating you.'

'Good, I don't want him coming anywhere near me! I've picked up a few tricks of my own over the past few seasons and I reckon I could take him.'

'You probably could Scar, and mainly because he would let you.'

Becky said no more, instead she just let Scar calm down again and think about what had been said. Later that evening, while Scar was still tingling strangely from his extended treatment, Silas ventured out into the yard. Scar's back immediately arched and his ears drew back. He left the safety of the chest for the open space of the yard. Protection charm or no, he was not about to be cornered by Silas in any box. Silas however, did not approach him, instead he simply sat on a small stump of wood by the back door and made himself comfortable.

'I don't suppose there's anything I can say that would set your mind at ease, my old friend?'

Scar's body language was the only reply he needed. Silas then apologised most sincerely for his past behaviour and for what he tried to do to him but this met with little reaction. Silas knew that there would be no quick fix for what he had done if there was any way to fix it at all. All he could do was to explain what had led him to that dark place and how wretched he felt about his past behaviour.

Day after day, as Becky drew out Scar's treatment to give them the time they needed, Silas would come outside and just sit and talk to Scar. He began at the very beginning and explained how ungratefully he had accepted the family legacy and how he had thought only of himself when first experimenting with magic. Silas still did not possess the natural gift of animal language that Becky had but he had learned enough for Scar to understand most of what he was trying to say and Silas could judge Scar's reaction to his words quite well, although Scar was still of a mind to remain silent.

Days passed and Silas gradually opened his heart to his old friend and Scar, hard and sceptical as he was, could not ignore the honesty of what he was hearing. Silas expected nothing in return. He simply told it as it had been for him, from the darkest depths of his anger and despair to the happiness that Becky had brought into his life through her patience and trust. As Silas explained the events of the past years, Scar wondered if he could have shown more patience with Silas or if there was anything he could have done to change his ways. However, Scar realised that Silas *had* to fall as low as he had done, before he could turn back. It was in the darkest moment, when he had tried to evaporate his familiar that Silas realised just how far he had fallen. Scar also realised a painful truth and that was that he *had* to be there for that moment. It was neither by accident nor coincidence that he was the biggest and strongest familiar his colony had ever produced. He had needed to be strong to stand up to Silas' darker side, he had needed an equally strong faith in magic too if he was to survive an evaporation spell cast in anger. That had been his roll, at least the first part of it. Turning Silas back, had been his sister's task. Becky, with her unique outlook on life and an understanding of animals not seen since Ezra Grimdyke, was the unusual solution to the troubled Grimdyke line.

'Everything happens for a reason,' Scar thought.

Some days later, as Silas drew nearer to the present with his account, there came a significant change. Silas was telling Scar what little he could remember about the time he fell into the mire that left him close to death. At this point Scar left the cover of the tea chest and sat in the middle of the space that had separated them for so long. Silas made no change in his manner or position, he simply continued with the account of his recovery and his time with Becky.

By the end of the second week, when Becky brought out some fresh kibble for Scar, she found him sitting at Silas' feet listening to his description of the firework display and the reception it got from the villagers. Septimouse was feeling brave enough to join them this day and sat listening to the tale from the comfort of Silas' top pocket.

'Tell him about the mouse fireworks,' Septimouse said excitedly.

Silas explained how they had created fireworks to represent each of them that night, mice, cats and even one of himself. 'Especially smiley so as not to frighten the children,' Silas added a little self-consciously.

'Now tell him about Shceschill,' Septimouse laughed.

As Silas recalled their recent visit by the llama *come* lawn-sprinkler, Scar found himself understanding Silas better. Over the past few days, Scar had listened to an account of the wizard's life and lived it with him as he spoke. He had felt the despair Silas had felt and seen the regret in his face even as the watery tale of Cecil unfolded. Scar now sat at Silas' side and after a brief moment of hesitation, even allowed Silas to stroke his head. During this time, Becky had been at the front of the croft, with a girl from the village. She had brought her cat along which had been suffering from bad skin and fur-loss. Quite used to being seen by Becky on her own the girl and her cat had waited patiently as Becky first prepared the potion, then applied it to the cat's back and tail.

'This is most undignified,' the cat complained haughtily as Becky smeared on the potion.

'Worse than having a back like a piece of toast and a tail like a twig?' Becky replied.

Hearing this, the girl laughed.

'Wait, you can understand felish?'

'Yes, a little. Ethan tried to teach me but there wasn't much time before he left. I picked up most of it myself, after he had taught me how to listen properly. My name is April and this silly bristly thing is Sebastian. I don't really speak felish so I hope you can understand me alright.'

'April, Seb, I think there is someone you both should meet. Follow me.'

Becky led the girl and her cat around to the back of the croft. April recognised Scar as soon as she saw him. Scar looked up and meowed, it was the first real sound he had made since his arrival. April walked over to Scar and held out her hand. Scar sniffed it then gave it a quick lick.

'You do remember me!' April said.

'I think I owe you my thanks too, for providing Scar with a safe means of carrying his potion ingredients,' Silas said to April, 'but tell me, how is it you understand cats so well?'

'Ethan … he seemed to think it would be a good idea if I learned felish. I didn't understand why at the time but I think I'm beginning to,' April replied.

'I think I'm beginning to understand better myself now and I don't think that any of us are here by coincidence. What would everyone say to a hot drink and something to eat?' Silas opened the croft door to welcome his guests in but then turned to Scar and added, 'Of course, I'll bring yours outside, if you would prefer.'

At that moment, Scar was preoccupied talking to Sebastian about the green gunk on his tail and back.

'I had a grooming problem,' Sebastian explained a little awkwardly, 'probably diet related. My servant here thought I should get it looked at.'

April smiled. She may not have been fluent in felish but she knew her cat very well.

'You can get rid of that now if you like,' Becky said to Sebastian at which point he shook himself sending a small cloud of green dust into the air.

As Sebastian followed April into the croft, he was followed in turn by a suddenly very curious Scar. He was studying Sebastian's tail and back with great interest, after which he looked accusingly at Becky.

'How is it that you cured Seb's problem in a matter of minutes but it took you two weeks to cure mine?'

'It took you two weeks to cure your problem with Silas,' she replied, knowingly, 'your fur problem could have been cured at any time.'

While Scar and Becky continued to tease each other, they kept walking and without realising it, they were soon inside the small croft. April and Sebastian had something to eat and drink at the kitchen table. Even Septimouse was feeling a little braver and had started to eat a small biscuit given to him by Silas. Seeing that the mouse had at last surfaced and realising that he was now surrounded by three cats, Becky gave him a small twig from the besom-broom that had been first dipped in protection potion.

'If you begin to feel nervous again or either Sebastian or Scar get too inquisitive, just wave that stick at them, they'll get the message.' Septimouse practised a few swings with his new wand, which seemed to reassure him and then his attention returned to the talk around the table and his biscuit.

Scar stood in the sitting room where he paused for a moment as his mind wandered back to his last day with *old* Silas. He looked at the floor where his sleeping box had stood. The stone floor was now repaired and Becky's smart hatbox replaced his evaporated sleeping box but he could still clearly picture the scene in his mind's eye.

'I guess more than just the floor has been mended over the past few seasons,' Scar said to Becky.

'You could say that but you needed to come back to the croft before the last of the damage could be repaired,' Becky replied. 'Now, come and sit with us and tell me all about the collecting bag and April.'

CHAPTER TWENTY
Candra

Life at Highfell Croft felt uncommonly appropriate. For the first time in a very long time, everyone felt as if they were in the right place and for the right reasons. Scar decided to stay on with Becky for the remainder of her term with Silas, that way he could share in the duties and catch up a little on the magic he sorely missed.

One quiet morning, when there had been few visitors to disturb the peace and quiet, Becky had found some much-needed time to go through some of Silas' old spell and potion books. All the time, Septimouse watched her closely from his high vantage point next to the potions cupboard. He may have been small but his beady eyes rarely missed a thing that happened in the croft.

'You're up to something, aren't you?' the mouse enquired shrewdly.

'Only a very *small* something,' Becky replied cheekily, before announcing, 'Ah, here it is. I knew it had to be here somewhere.'

She then set down the book again and strolled casually over to where Silas and Scar were sitting, talking. Then, as Silas was explaining some of the finer points of elixir brewing, Becky stood squarely in front of Scar and fixed him with a slightly cross-eyed stare. She was trying to remember the exact wording of a particularly complicated spell … and then she sneezed.

'FISHOO!'

'Oh, great sis! Thanks for sharing that!' but as the sparkling cloud settled around him, Scar realised that something very special might have just happened. 'Sis, what have you done?'

'Just given you something you should have had years ago.'

'What a bad cold!' Scar laughed, only half meaning it.

'No, a protection spell, of course.'

'You can do that? I thought only a wizard could cast a protection spell over a familiar … and I'm not even a real familiar am I, you are now.'

Silas smiled, 'I'm not *exactly* sure what Becky is but she is more than capable of casting a protection spell or any other spell for that matter, if she puts her mind to it. As for you not being a real familiar, that's not a position you can back out of just like that so the job is still yours … yours and Becky's *jointly* … if you still want it.'

'And with that spell in place, you will leave here as fit and young as the day you arrived,' Becky added, rubbing her nose.

'But I don't want to forget everything after …'

'I think,' Silas considered thoughtfully, 'that as with Nightfire, Luna and Raven, you and Becky will remember quite a lot of your time here. My only regret now is that I could not cast a protection spell over you, Becky. It would only be right to return to you the years spent in the service of a most difficult wizard.'

'I have my own protection charm …'

'… As far as self gain allows,' Silas, Septimouse and Scar chanted in reply.

'Yes, and that will do for me. If I want any more I'll just have to invent an anti-wrinkle cream that *actually* works!'

'Well, I've said it before and I'll say it again, now that we're all together at last, we make a pretty strange family but I wouldn't have it any other way.'

Barren Moor looked far less bleak now somehow, as did life at Highfell. Silas and his odd family soon settled into a comfortable and satisfying routine together. Silas studied from his family's old potion books, Becky from the spell books while Scar and Septimouse peered over both their shoulders trying things out for themselves in any free moment they had. Becky had realised some time earlier that Septimouse was anything but an ordinary mouse and a possible link with Ethan she could not quite explain. She also knew that it would be a safe and a wise move to equip the small rodent with his own wand. In the same way that Raven realised the potential power in the twigs from the besom-broom so too did Becky, allowing Septimouse his first opportunity to try real magic firsthand. Scar was a quick learner and took to magic every bit as well as Becky expected him to, and soon they were able to hold small magic championships with transformation, evaporation and retrieval spells all demonstrated to a high degree of skill. Silas' potions were now almost as advanced as Becky's and they all marvelled at her advancing skills of sneeze-casting. With a slightly cross-eyed look and a sudden '*FISHOO*', Becky could perform almost any magic trick in the book and even a few that were not yet in there.

For the purpose of the challenge, they placed on the table a large wax candle and then they each took turns in transforming it into a different likeness. Septimouse chose to turn it into a block of cheese, Becky created a perfect likeness of a fish, Scar then turned the fish into a small mouse, which made Septimouse squeak and immediately doubt Scar's intentions. Finally, Silas blew a potion over the wax mouse, which turned it into a fine meal for each of them, and at that point, the competition was declared a draw. Scar and Becky had fresh fishy-kibble, Septimouse had a nice nugget of mixed cereals and Silas his favourite pie with some crunchy chips.

Silas assured Becky that as it was a magical pie, none of her animal friends would be inside it.

The next morning, as Silas watched for their first visitor, he noticed something curious heading their way across the moor and then began the strangest game of twenty questions. With Silas in the window, the others tried to guess who their latest visitor could be.

'A llama!' Septimouse called out with a chuckle.

'No, definitely not a llama.'

'A whole *herd* of llamas!' Becky added laughing even more.

'Not *quite* that big,' Silas replied, rubbing the window clear to gain a better view.

'A group of villagers with posh cats,' Scar suggested as he joined in the guessing.

'No, I don't think it's anyone from Skellside.' Silas was at a loss to explain this latest arrival.

By this time, everyone present was at the window trying to see what was coming their way. Down the narrow lane, completely undeterred by the tall grass and weeds blocking the old road, came a small van. To be precise, it was an old campervan. As they watched, they realised that something even more peculiar was happening. The weeds and brambles in its path were actually disappearing before the van ever reached them.

'Now that's something you don't see everyday!' Silas declared.

The van continued to glide towards the croft with the weeds dissolving and vanishing in its way. Eventually, it reached the gate into the adjacent field and as the van approached, the gate swung open allowing it to pull in.

'That's *definitely* not something you see everyday!' Silas by now had his wand in hand and so too did Septimouse. Even

Becky appeared to be preparing a defensive potion, should one be needed. Scar however, was still watching with keen interest.

'I know I'm new to all this but that is definitely magical, that's no ordinary … whatever that giant box *thing* is.'

'I think they're called campers and no, it's far from normal,' Silas replied.

'I'm not sensing any dark magic,' Becky explained, much to everyone's surprise. 'But there is very strong magic coming from inside.'

As they continued to watch, the van appeared to settle into place in the corner of the field, after which it immediately began to expand. First, the roof lifted to twice its original height, and then the sides expanded. It was almost as if the van was taking a deep relaxing breath at the end of a long journey. To their great surprise, when it had finished growing, it had expanded to the same size as Highfell Croft.

'Well, whoever they are they certainly have a unique form of transportation,' Silas said in admiration.

'What do you think they want?' Septimouse asked from his pocket lookout position.

'I think we're about to find out.'

As Silas spoke, the side door of the now cottage-sized van, opened and a brightly dressed young woman stepped out. After brushing her hands once over her long skirt, all the creases caused by the long journey vanished and the fabric shone like peacock feathers in the morning sun.

'I think it's going to be one of those days,' Silas said quietly, 'the kind that only comes around once in a blue moon.'

The young woman then took out what looked to be a small, ornate wand and waved it at the roof of the van. This caused a satellite dish and a small, smoking chimney to spring out. One further swirling gesture from her wand appeared to cut and clear the long grass from around the van after which she tucked it away in the waistband of her skirt. After pausing to pull a purple beret from the air, she set off towards the croft.

'I think we're about to have a visitor,' Silas explained as he began tidying away loose newspapers and shopping receipts.

Becky glanced around the room and shook her head.

'Maybe just this once. After all, it's not just for me … *FISHOO*! That's much better.'

The main room and kitchen were now clean, tidy, presentable and ready for their mysterious new guest. Just then, the front door resounded with a solid 'rat-a-tat-tat' then they heard someone outside say, 'Silly me but you don't use the front door!' Then the footsteps retreated around to the back of the croft, to the back yard and then up to the kitchen door.

'Rat-tat-a-tat-tat … tat-tat.'

Silas opened the door to find himself confronted by a young woman dressed in a smart postal delivery worker's uniform.

'Delivery for Grimdyke!' she announced cheerily.

'I'm Silas Grimdyke but … weren't you wearing a brightly coloured dress a moment ago?'

Undeterred and still smiling broadly, the girl checked the label again.

'Of course you are, I'd recognise you anywhere … I see you wield a Hemlock wand. I hope you have its darker side well under control,' the girl eyed both the wand and Silas warily.

'Yes, I have *now* … but how did …' Silas began to say.

'Good, I'm so glad that little problem has been sorted out.' Whoever the girl was, she seemed surprisingly well informed with events at Highfell. 'Now, back to the delivery. This is for *Becky* Grimdyke, *familiar* to Silas Grimdyke.'

Hearing her name mentioned, Becky stepped forward, although she could not imagine why anyone should be sending anything to her.

'I'm Becky,' she replied in felish.

'So very pleased to finally meet you Becky. Yes, full glossy black coat and small white crescent on the chest, how could you be anyone else. This is for you.'

The girl then placed a small box on the floor in front of her. It was wrapped in orange paper and tied with a green ribbon.

'Well, I expect you should open it,' Silas urged.

Becky cautiously tugged at the ribbon with her claws and pulled until the bow gave way. Then, being a cat and naturally curious, she immediately began pulling off the bright wrapping. Not knowing quite what to expect next, she then teased open the box lid.

'It's a potion … and there's a label attached to the bottle.' Becky read the message.

Dear Becky,

I apologise for not delivering this in person but it comes with all my gratitude and appreciation for a job well done. I am sure by now that you have taken care of your brother's magical needs and so this is a special thank you just for you.

Ethan Grimdyke

P.S. Please explain to my son Silas, how proud I am of him and tell him that I never doubted for one minute that he had it within him to become a great wizard.

Until we meet again … at the turning of the next page.

Becky looked at Silas and then back to the bottle, unsure what she should do next.

'Turn over the label,' the young woman encouraged her.

On the reverse side of the saffron yellow label were written the words, "Shangri-La Serum".

'Ethan thought you might need it because your work here is not yet over,' the girl explained.

'But what does it do? I don't remember seeing the potion in any of Ethan or Ezra's books.' Becky tapped the iridescent purple bottle and the liquor inside twinkled and shone.

'If you choose to drink it, it will suspend the passage of time for you, for as long as you serve the Wizards Grimdyke. Think of it as an everlasting seven-year protection charm. Only when or if you choose to return to your feral life, will you begin to age like a normal cat. There is one thing I should warn you about however and that is that the potion is in no way an invulnerability potion. Such potions are brief and not without side effects. This serum is the result of the highest form of white magic and serves only to assist. It will keep you safe from all but the darkest of magic or the greatest of maladies but as you will be in the service of a wizard, no self gain penalties apply.'

Becky thought about it for a moment.

'You say my work here is not over?'

'If you accept the proposition I have been asked to put to you.'

Becky thought only briefly before drinking the potion and after shuddering for a second then going slightly wobbly-legged, she announced that she felt fine.

'You won't find this brew written in any books because the writing of it changes the ingredients and the effect. Oh, you may think it has been written correctly but as soon as you turn away, the recipe changes and usually with most unfortunate results. You see, this is one of a special group of potions that are protected by an unbreakable mixlexia spell. It protects the potions from duplication or theft and the recipe can only be retained in the mind of a great wizard … or sometimes a white mage.'

Becky looked from the bottle to their strange new visitor and narrowed her eyes.

'Are you a white mage? Only I sense many creatures in you and many eyes.'

On hearing Becky's remark Scar and Silas exchanged puzzled looks but Becky knew what she meant and it appeared so too did their visitor.

'I've worn this guise too long now, do you mind if I change back to something more casual?' After removing the small and very ornately carved wand from her belt, the young woman drew it carefully over her image, as if squeegeeing a window but instead of a clean pane, it revealed the brightly dressed visitor that had stepped from the campervan.

'That's better. Now, as I already know all of you it's only fair that you know a little more about me. My name is Candra and as I said before, I am so very glad to finally meet you all. Now let me see, I believe the fine big tom at your side, Silas, who has yet to speak, must be Whitescar or do you prefer Scar? So that just leaves one other, I think.'

At this point, Septimouse made his appearance, poking his head out of Silas' top pocket and as they watched him, everyone present was convinced that he winked at Candra but no one was *quite* sure enough to mention it at the time.

'How are you Septimouse, well I trust?'

Septimouse squeaked his agreement, much to the surprise of all and from her reply, it was immediately apparent that Candra was fluent in quite a few animal languages.

'I know you must have a thousand questions to ask … I know I have so why don't you all come round to my little van and we can have dinner. Sid should have it all in hand by now.'

Silas and the other members of the Grimdyke household immediately agreed and they followed Candra back to her temporary home in the next field. It would probably be true to say that at that moment, the strong feline curiosity of Scar and Becky was more than matched by that of Silas as they neared the unusual campervan, and all but Septimouse were clearly eager to see inside it.

As they approached, the first thing they all wondered was how it had been able to navigate the narrow lane so easily. It appeared to be quite a bit larger in width, even without the new extensions, with them the van was easily the equal of Highfell Croft in size. Silas then noticed the footpath that led to the front door of the mobile house and the fine array of flowers growing alongside it. The campervan appeared to have been there for years, instead of minutes.

'There are *some* loopholes in the "no personal gain" rule then?' Silas observed.

'Any improvements are for the benefit of all,' Candra replied slightly impishly, showing her willingness to test any boundaries. 'I just make a point of never being selfish and things seem to work out.'

'Always a good rule to live by,' Silas smiled.

Just before they entered the van, Septimouse squeaked again, drawing their attention to the plaque on the door.

"SID-RAT" it announced, in fine carved letters.

'No, no rats inside, Septimouse but it was a rat that named it. He said it was appropriate because it looked a lot smaller inside than it did from the outside but you'll see what a strange sense of humour he had when you come in.'

No sooner had they stepped through the doorway than they were all backing outside again to check the van's exterior.

'This isn't right … *is* it?' Silas asked bemused.

'Whatever do you mean,' Candra replied falsely.

'Well … it's *too* big … isn't it?'

231

'No, just about right … for a *magical* house. Make yourselves at home and feel free to have a good look round, just try not to get lost.'

Despite the more modern and mechanical exterior of a campervan, the inside looked more *tent*-like … a very large and multi-roomed tent. Becky immediately set off at a trot to explore. On the ground floor, she found four large rooms including a fully fitted kitchen, where the dinner smelled almost ready. In the corner of the main room, she then noticed a spiral staircase that led to an upper floor and, even more intriguingly, it even appeared to lead down to a basement. By now, Becky was in full-blown investigation mode and she began by racing up the winding stairs. At the top, she found even more rooms, a bedroom, small library, an entire room set aside for potions and spells, and a small balcony or viewing platform with splendid views over the surrounding moor to Skellside.

Having just whetted her appetite for more investigation, something new began creating a very real appetite in her, this time for food. The smell of dinner wafted up the stairs to her and it was intoxicating. Its mouth-watering aroma soon had Becky downstairs again and seated around the large round dining table with the others. Then, as the last of the self-stirring pans finished its set task, Candra announced that dinner was ready.

There was a fine pie with vegetables and lashings of gravy for Silas and herself, pan-fried chicken for Scar and some poached fish for Becky. For Septimouse, Candra had created a special cereal and nut energy-bar that smelled of summer fruits. Although Scar tucked into his food with great relish, he did remember to look a little guilty for Becky's sake, explaining that he would try the fish another day.

When the main meal and the strawberries and ice-cream dessert were finished, Candra directed the dirty crockery into the sink with her wand. In response, the small sink obligingly expanded to take all she sent its way after which, the scrubbing brushes and mops did the rest.

'While the dishes are washing themselves, let's go upstairs to the balcony where we can talk.'

Candra led everyone to the seating area with views over Barren Moor, where they sat and began to relax. First Candra sent for refreshments all round, magically of course and when everyone had something to drink, she took a last look over the moor before turning to Silas and the others.

'It's hard to believe, looking across the quiet fell now, that … but I should not say too much, too soon. Right, first things first. I can see you already have a fine grasp of healing, rudimentary protection charms and potions but as you can all see from my *little* van, there is much you still need to learn.'

As Candra talked, Becky studied her with head tilted to one side.

'I sense that Becky already suspects that Ethan has sent me and she is right of course. I come from an old magical family, far to the south of here and I have come to help … *if* you will permit me. My family specialises in spreading word of the old ways, keeping it alive in the right kinds of families. Healing and scrying for lost objects are two sides of magic that most people are allowed to see but there is a third. This side is more … *unexpected* and far less likely to be understood by non-magical folk but it is this side that I have been sent to teach you.

'Silas, you have more than proved yourself a true Grimdyke but in doing so you have placed your name openly on the map and it will not be allowed to rest there untested. Every great transition within a family line brings with it its own challenge; yours has been seen and it draws near.' Candra then turned to Becky and for a moment, even appeared to be looking inside her, rather than at her. 'I already know that when you drink from your bowl, you do more than satisfy your thirst ... am I right? You use your water bowl as a scrying pool to answer the growing number of questions you feel inside.'

'I thought you stared a long time into your water before drinking,' Silas remarked.

Then it was Silas' turn to be considered by Candra.

'And Silas, what of *your* desires? You long to be a great wizard like your father ... no, I am wrong, you long to be a great *man* like your father and earn the respect of the villagers. Good, then the last trace of jealousy is behind you and I have arrived just at the right moment. Together, we will complete your training ... so that each of you can become all that you are ... and for what is to come, you will need to be *very* well prepared. Those with the gift of sight have seen something of your futures and of the dark forces that will soon arrive to test your resolve but do not despair, that will not be for some ...' Candra checked the very odd-looking watch on her wrist, '... well, not *tonight* anyway. We have much work to do and less time than I would have liked in which to do it but that's often the way it is. Oh, but now I'm beginning to alarm you. There's no need for alarm yet ... there'll be plenty of time for that later. First comes the good part. What you are about to learn will blow your socks off and for those without socks, hang on to your whiskers!'